Jack Starett grasped her wrist, fighting to keep his grip gentle...

Somehow he managed to keep the emotion tearing through him out of his voice. The scar on her wrist...so help him, it looked like... "Looks like something mean took a bite out of you. How'd it happen?"

"I was young," Andrea said. "I can't—er—don't remember."

Didn't or couldn't? Jack cautioned himself against the excitement he felt stirring in his gut. Was his obsession with a long-lost little girl working overtime?

She chuckled nervously. "May I please have my bracelet back?"

Very casually, Jack said, "Sure." As he returned the jewelry, his gaze landed on her mouth, and the urge to kiss her jarred him. But it was her, all right. The woman he'd been tracking for years. The woman who—as a child—had witnessed a murder.

MARRY ME,
Cowboy

MIDNIGHT
COWBOY

Adrianne Lee

Secrets!

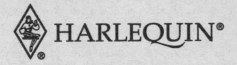

HARLEQUIN®

TORONTO • NEW YORK • LONDON
AMSTERDAM • PARIS • SYDNEY • HAMBURG
STOCKHOLM • ATHENS • TOKYO • MILAN • MADRID
PRAGUE • WARSAW • BUDAPEST • AUCKLAND

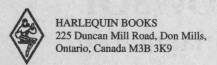

HARLEQUIN BOOKS
225 Duncan Mill Road, Don Mills,
Ontario, Canada M3B 3K9

ISBN 0-373-65353-0

MIDNIGHT COWBOY

Copyright © 1996 by Adrianne Lee Undsderfer

This edition published by arrangement with Harlequin Books S.A.

® and TM are trademarks of the publisher. Trademarks indicated with ® are registered in the United States Patent and Trademark Office, the Canadian Trade Marks Office and in other countries.

www.eHarlequin.com

Printed in U.S.A.

ADRIANNE LEE

When asked why she wanted to write romance fiction, Adrianne Lee replied, "I wanted to be Doris Day when I grew up. You know, singing my way through one wonderful romance after another. And I did. I fell in love with and married my high-school sweetheart and became the mother of three beautiful daughters. Family and love are very important to me and I hope you enjoy the way I weave them through my stories." Adrianne also loves hearing from her readers. She is happy to write back and can be reached at: Adrianne Lee, P.O. Box 3835, Sequim, WA 98382. Please enclose a SASE if you'd like a response.

Please address questions and book requests to:
Harlequin Reader Service
U.S.: 3010 Walden Ave., P.O. Box 1325, Buffalo, NY 14269
Canadian: P.O. Box 609, Fort Erie, Ont. L2A 5X3

For the girls who have made and continue to make my life richer every day: Kim and Karin and Krissa. Brandi and Savannah. Judy and Mary Alice and Nadine.

Special thanks to Mary Birdsill of Madison County Sheriff's Department, Virginia City, Montana. Jerry Brown & Larry Jensen—Maple Valley Fire Department. (King County Fire Department #43.)

Prologue

"Leandra has suffered a terrible shock, Mrs. Woodworth." The lady psychiatrist spoke just above a whisper. "No five-year-old should have to go through what that poor child has in the past three days. Watching her parents murdered. Almost being murdered herself."

Eloise Woodworth felt ten years older than her fifty-one years as she glanced at her granddaughter, who was sleeping on the hospital bed across the room. Her gaze fell on the bandages covering the little girl's left wrist. The doctor said the three gashes weren't infected, but they would leave an unsightly scar.

It was the scars that couldn't be seen that worried Eloise. "Will she recover?"

The doctor's expression grew kindly. "Right now, hysterical amnesia is keeping Leandra from recalling the face of the murderer."

The knot in Eloise's stomach tightened. "Are you saying she might remember at any time who her Nightmare Man is?"

The doctor paused. "It's a possibility we should anticipate."

"But he knows she can identify him."

"Yes, and that's why the police are just outside this room. But Leandra can't stay here forever. Have you thought of how you'll protect her when she's released?"

Grief over the loss of her precious son and daughter-in-law and fear for Lee Lee had controlled her mind and body for the past few days. She hadn't thought at all. Only wandered through each day in a numbed haze. But this doctor was right. She must consider the safety of her granddaughter. "I guess I haven't. I'm not a wealthy woman. I can't afford round-the-clock bodyguards, and the police aren't going to go on protecting us forever, are they?"

The doctor shook her head.

"I guess I have some thinking to do."

The doctor left, and Eloise moved to the bed. Lee Lee's dark brown hair spilled across the pillow in chocolate ribbons. Her eyes were closed, their dark lashes lacy against cheeks as pale as the sheets on which she lay. Eloise brushed a loving hand tenderly across the child's forehead.

Lee Lee was all she had now. *She* was all Lee Lee had. Somehow she had to insure the little girl's continued well-being. Somehow the police had to solve this case quickly.

And if they didn't?

She shuddered at the awful possibility. The sound of the door opening behind her brought her jerking around. A stranger, a lanky man with stringy blond hair, stood in the doorway. He wore a wrinkled brown suit with an orange-and-white-polka-dot tie. "Who are you?"

The stranger stepped into the room.

Automatically Eloise moved in front of the bed, shielding Lee Lee. "Where's Officer Rawlins?"

"Don't worry, granny. I'm harmless."

The stranger grinned, a lousy lopsided smile that Eloise assumed was meant to disarm her. It raised the hackles on her neck and sent a bolt of terror through her. "Where is Officer Rawlins?"

"Rawlins has been out there for hours." The man walked toward her. "All that coffee, well, a man has to take an occasional break. I told him I'd stand guard while he relieved himself.''

Eloise's nostrils flared with fear. Was this the man who'd killed her son and daughter-in-law? The man little Lee Lee called Nightmare Man? Her pulse accelerated. She groped behind her for the buzzer to alert the nurse's station. It eluded her. Instead, she wheeled around and grabbed her purse, quickly reaching inside for the Beretta. ''If Rawlins left you on guard, what are you doing in here?''

''I just wanted to ask the little girl a couple of questions.'' He produced a camera from his suit pocket and raised it at her, snapping a shot off. The bright flash of light blinded Eloise.

Blinking, she pulled the gun from her purse and waved it at him. ''Get out!''

''Hey, don't shoot me. I'm a reporter.'' The stringy-haired man reared back, his hands raised in protest. ''Moses Arlington with the *Missoula Sentinel*.''

''I don't care if you're with the *New York Times*—if you don't get yourself out of this room within two seconds I'm going to blow a hole through you the size of the Conrey mine.''

''Hey, hang on, granny. I don't mean any harm. I just want an interview.''

''Now.'' Eloise took a step toward him.

With his eyes wide and his face ashen, Moses backed toward the door. ''Okay, granny. Your point is taken. I'm leaving. Don't shoot.''

The door swung open and shut. Eloise's chest heaved and her hands began to tremble. She waited four seconds, then hurried to the door and peered into the hall. Moses Arlington was disappearing into an elevator. There was no sign of Officer Rawlins. Fury swept her. Damned police. Promised Lee Lee would have round-the-clock protection. Some protection.

Eloise understood now that she was the only one committed

to keeping her granddaughter safe. The task would require some drastic measures, sacrifices such as she'd never before made in her life. But she'd learned something vital these past days: nothing was as important as loved ones.

Material goods could be replaced. Lee Lee could not.

She hurried to the bed and scooped up the sleeping child. Even though she'd been bathed, a hint of smoke clung to Lee Lee. Rawlins had not returned. Eloise wrapped her tightly in the hospital blanket, carried her down the deserted hall to the stairs and out to the parking lot.

So much for security.

The moon was as full as a supper plate overhead. ''Montana fool's moon,'' she muttered as she hastened to her trusty white Lincoln, the one luxury she'd ever indulged herself in. ''Pray God, we're leaving the fools behind.''

Safely inside the car's spacious confines, she settled Lee Lee on the aged leather seat beside her. After making certain no one was following, she drove out of Butte and onto Interstate 90, heading for the Idaho border.

Beside her, the little girl moaned as though from a bad dream.

Eloise caressed her cheek. ''Don't you worry, my precious Lee Lee. Gram's making certain Nightmare Man will never find you.''

Chapter One

Something more sinister than one of Montana's freak May snowstorms was brewing this lousy afternoon. Jack Starett, Jr., knew it the minute he saw his ex-boss, Wallingford Lester, the editor of the *Butte Sun*, driving up the lane to his ranch house. Trouble. In capital letters.

If he had a brain in his head, he wouldn't open the door to the man. Arguing with himself over this matter, Jack watched Wally hunch his shoulders and make for the stoop. Wind whined through the cottonwood trees, battering against him, riffling his thick grayed crew cut and whipping his unbuttoned overcoat away from his stocky body like a flapping flag.

Deciding it wouldn't be neighborly to ignore Wally's frantic knocking, Jack yanked the door open, then filled its frame. At thirty-three he presented an imposing figure, an attribute he considered an asset and often used to advantage. His gaze riveted on the manila envelope Wally held to his chest like a shield.

Clutching his coat together and effectively covering the envelope, Wally, a devout flatterer, grinned at him. Jack braced himself for the outrageous compliment that was sure to follow. Wally didn't disappoint. "I declare, Starett, you're a sinfully handsome devil, even in overalls and a ratty flannel shirt."

Jack gave his unkempt black hair an impatient rake with

his long fingers, then scrubbed his whiskered jaw. "Yeah, like a green-eyed grizzly. Save the bull, Wally. Cut to the chase, I'm mighty busy."

Wally's expression grew stony. "Surely you can spare *me* a few minutes?"

As curious as Jack was about what had brought Wally here unannounced, he was more anxious about the problems he already knew. His gaze skipped to the black afternoon sky, to the pastures spread down the knoll, to his restless cattle. It was biting cold out there. They could lose a good number of new calves, a loss Starett Ranch could ill afford. Their restaurants had taken a beating during this recent recession. "Max is expecting me out in the north field, but you're welcome to come in and wait until I get back. Stick around for dinner."

"Your brother-in-law has run this ranch a good long while on his own." There was an uncommon acerbic bite to Wally's tone. He shrugged deeper into his overcoat. "He'll manage a few minutes more. It's important."

That much Jack had already guessed. Wally wouldn't be here otherwise. Sure he was going to regret it, Jack said, "All right. Come in."

He shut the door on the wind, strode toward the open-beamed living room with its quarry rock fireplace and motioned toward a chair, but Wally shook his head.

From behind the closed kitchen door beyond came the sounds of Ruth Starett, Jack's mother, and Jonna, his older sister—Max's wife—humming softly as they prepared dinner. The aromas of baking bread and roasting pork scented the air.

"In the den." Wally spoke low.

"Okay." Jack's frown deepened and a bad feeling swept him as he led Wally to the den, where until recently Jack had plotted and honed his obsession with finding the man who'd murdered his father, Jack Starett, Sr. Since his eighteenth birthday he'd used the den as a plot room, filled with every scrap of information he'd thought pertinent. He'd been obsessed with finding and bringing the man to justice, but, although he'd turned into one of the best investigative reporters in the country—as his father had been before him—he'd never found the man he sought.

Thank God he'd walked away when he had—before the obsession consumed any more of his life. He closed the door, shutting off the homey sounds of the women in the kitchen.

His ex-boss looked taken aback by the changes in the den.

"What's the matter, Wally? I thought you'd approve of the redecorating." He'd turned the den into a reflection of the good things in his and Jack senior's investigative reporting days. Photographs and news clippings, prized periods of both men's careers, adorned the walls.

"Nice, Junior. Nice." Wally's gaze settled on the dry sink, on the liquor bottles lined up on it like soldiers awaiting instructions. "I'll have Black Velvet. You'd better fix yourself some, too."

Strictly to be courteous, Jack complied, and a moment later handed a tumbler to the editor, who now sat in one of the wingback leather chairs facing Jack's desk. He'd removed his overcoat and the envelope was once again in evidence, this time on his lap.

Jack carried his own drink to the other side of the desk and dropped into the castered chair that had long ago molded itself to his contours. He couldn't get comfortable. Prickles, starting at the base of his spine, inched upward. More than likely the storm. Still… Wally seemed excited in the same way he always had been when a good story was breaking.

There'd been a time when that was all Jack needed to see to get excited, too. That was no longer the case. He had other concerns. His gaze swept to the window. The clouds seemed heavier. He had to get to Max. "I'm telling you right now, Wally, this better be damned important."

"It is, it is. You remember the Karen Bradley case?"

"Of course I do." He'd thought for sure Karen had been another of *his killer's* victims. But he'd been out of town at the time on another story, a couple of Olympic ice skaters run amuck. By the time he'd returned, the trail had grown cold, and an ornery police lieutenant had blocked everything he'd tried learning on his own time about the case. He sure as blazes didn't want to hear about it now. "Karen Bradley is old news. The police have arrested Gus Dillard for her murder. In fact, he's probably going to trial soon."

"Strange you should mention the trial." Wally's thick fingers curled the edge of the manila envelope on his lap. "Last Wednesday a police detective paid me a visit. The subject of her concern was the impending trial of Gus Dillard. She claims the man's been railroaded, that there are inconsistencies in the police investigation being overlooked in lieu of a speedy conviction."

"In other words, Gus Dillard is being allowed to slip through the cracks." Jack's boot tapped the floor in tune to the beat of the wind and the impatience stirring his blood. "It happens, Wally."

"That doesn't make it right." Wally pushed his glass onto the desk and placed the manila envelope beside it. "However, that alone wouldn't have brought me here."

Jack stared at the envelope. There was only one reason Wally would want to talk to him about the Karen Bradley case. He tossed back a swallow of whiskey. It burned a path to his belly. "This isn't just about Gus Dillard, is it?"

Wally grinned. "I've always said you were the smartest of the smartest, Junior."

"I ought to throw you out of here right now!" Jack snapped. "For the past fifteen years you've hounded me to let go of my obsession with Dad's murderer. News flash—I have. Accept it, deal with it."

Wally shook his head. "No chance, son. This is one story

I can't ignore, and you're the one reporter who can pull it off.''

"Wally, I quit. Remember? I'm not a reporter anymore, I'm a rancher.''

"We'll see if you still feel that way after you know what I know.''

Wally knew his weaknesses too well. Despite his fear of the obsession, Jack could not deny interest. He tensed, struggling against it. He had too much to lose, had already lost too much. They stared at one another for a long count, ticked off by the moaning wind. Finally Jack asked, "What do you know, Wally?''

Wally petted the envelope as if it were a kitten.

Jack's mouth was dry. "Have you found Leandra Woodworth?'' It was probably too much to hope that the little girl who'd escaped the house fire in which both her parents had perished might actually turn up.

The two articles Jack Senior had written about her and her tragedy were filed away in the attic now, but every word was etched in his mind. If only his dad had left it at that, just covered the story instead of getting involved. He should have taken his cue from the little girl. The trauma of what she'd witnessed had robbed her memory of all but one name— Nightmare Man. As far as anyone knew, she was the only living soul who could identify the man he was after, the man who'd killed her parents and his father. "Has she turned up after all this time?''

Wally pressed his lips together. "No. Her grandmother did a bang-up job of covering her tracks. No one's ever found her. That's not to say we couldn't now. We could contact 'Unsolved Mysteries.' They'd probably find her in a heartbeat. She'd be twenty-five, and with that distinctive scar on her wrist and those unusually colored eyes of hers—''

"Have you lost your mind? How can you even consider putting the woman in such jeopardy?'' Shaking his head, Jack scraped his chair back. "I wouldn't be a party to anything like that."

"Will you please listen to me?"

"No, no." Panic exploded through Jack. He was being sucked in, his defenses dropping like fence posts in the wind. He started to stand. "I have to get going. Max is wait—"

"Please, Jack. A man's life is at stake."

Jack choked on the angry hatred buried deep inside him. Catching Nightmare Man had controlled his life for too long. Had ruined his life. He couldn't chase a ghost anymore. He wanted a wife. He wanted kids. He wanted a normal life. "You aren't counting right, Wally. Two men's lives are at stake—Gus Dillard's and mine."

"Just five minutes more," Wally pleaded.

In spite of his intention to do otherwise, Jack dropped back into his chair. Whiskey sloshed his wrist as he grabbed his glass. "I must be crazy."

Wally scooted to the edge of his chair and spoke rapidly. "How much do you know about the Karen Bradley case?"

A frustrated breath woofed from Jack. He'd left the paper right after Gus Dillard's arrest. "I wasn't assigned her story. Remember? But I know she was headed home from some summer job and she never made it."

Wally tapped the envelope.

Jack watched the tapping finger as if it were some kind of water torture he couldn't look away from. "What is that?"

"A complete copy of the police file on the Karen Bradley case."

He couldn't believe he'd heard right. "How did you—"

"*I* didn't. But once it was in my hands, I felt obligated to read it."

"Justify it any way you want, it's still illegal."

"Do you mean to say you aren't the least bit interested in what's in here?" He was tapping the envelope again.

Jack clenched the arms of his chair, his gaze riveted on the envelope. It had taken Gus Dillard's arrest to get through to him just how obsessed he was with Nightmare Man, to give up the obsession. And here was Wally telling him he might have given up too soon. His head ached as if some unknown sources were playing tug-of-war with his brain. The urge to see the file won. "Are you going to show me that report?"

Wally turned the envelope over and pinched the golden prongs that held the flap. He pulled a sheaf of papers free, but made no move to turn them over to Jack. "Inconsistency number one. The only fingerprints in Karen's car were Gus Dillard's." He slid a paper over to Jack.

Jack quickly read it, noting that it confirmed what Wally claimed. He suppressed his niggling curiosity. "So what?"

"So what?" Wally echoed. "So, why would a murderer wipe away his victim's fingerprints, then leave his own all over the place?"

The whiskey felt like lead in Jack's stomach. He shook his head. "Maybe Dillard was drunk...or high."

"Then why would he wipe her fingerprints away at all?"

Jack had no answer. It made no sense. But it was not his problem. Not yet. This time he did stand. "Wally, I can't get involved. I'm thirty-three. I've wasted my youth chasing every false lead that even smelled of Nightmare Man. I can't keep chasing a serial killer."

"You know darn well I never bought your serial killer notion. Never felt right—in here." He poked his ample stomach. "Until Karen Bradley—I don't think our guy has killed anyone since your dad."

Jack frowned. *Can Wally be right? Dear God, what am I doing?* Listening. Getting involved again. "Whether you're right or wrong no longer matters to me. I just want to forget it all."

There was a look of sympathetic understanding in Wally's brown eyes, but steel braced his words. "I hear you, son, truly

I do. But I can't forget about the Bradleys. Or Gus Dillard. In all good conscience, can you?''

God help him, he wanted to. He longed to be outside, on his horse, galloping through the pastures, the wind biting into his fevered flesh, venting the bellow of anguish blooming in his gut.

"Inconsistency number two," Wally said firmly. "Lack of cat hair in the car." He shoved another paper across the desk.

"What does cat hair have to do with Gus Dillard?"

"Everything and nothing." Wally stood, tucked the police report under one arm, crossed to the dry sink and returned with the bottle of Black Velvet. He refilled Jack's glass and gestured for him to drink.

Jack complied, wondering why the straight shots of booze hadn't dented the armor of tension gripping him.

Wally filled his own glass. "Karen adored cats. She adopted one while away from home. Named him Outlaw." His voice softened. "Her last letter to her parents was full of stories about Outlaw and how eager she was for them to meet him, as if the black-furred, yellow-eyed critter were their grandchild. That was back in September. At the time it was assumed Outlaw had fled the car when Gus came on the scene."

"But…?" Jack felt the pull of his obsession sucking at his willpower. His gaze shifted to the window. *Is that snow?* "Look, Wally…Max—"

Wally interrupted, pointing to the paper he'd just handed Jack. "That forensic report says the car was so clean you could have eaten off the seats. Not one cat hair."

Jack's attention jerked to Wally. No cat. Not even one cat hair in a car belonging to a confirmed cat lover. "What makes you think Nightmare Man is behind this?"

"This." Wally plunked down more papers. This bunch stapled. *The pathologist's report.* Cold washed over Jack as he read through the clinical findings.

"See that—on page three?" Wally's voice came out choked. He stretched toward Jack, flipped through the document until he came to the page he wanted, then poked his finger at the paper. "The police didn't tell the press about it, but although poor Karen's body had started to decompose, they could see that her neck was slashed with three, inch-long gashes, as—"

"As though she'd been clawed by a huge bird of prey." *Just like Dad.* A tremor rocked through Jack like an earthquake measuring nine point five on the Richter scale.

"But here's the kicker. Peterson did the story, visited the Bradleys and picked out some ditzy cheerleading photograph to run with his copy on Karen. When I visited the Bradleys this morning and saw this photograph I nearly had heart failure."

Jack grabbed the photo, turning it toward him. He might be staring at a picture of Marcy Woodworth, Leandra's mother. Jack whispered, "This is Karen Bradley?"

Wally nodded. "Spooky, isn't it?"

Despite his promises to himself, despite the misgivings beating a tattoo inside his achy head, Jack felt a tingle of excitement rising in his blood. "Where did Karen Bradley spend the summer?"

But he already knew the answer. The town where the Woodworths had lived…and died. Alder Gulch, Montana.

IT WAS AS IF she'd crossed a time threshold into the mid-1800s and landed right smack in a gold-boom town. Andrea Hart felt her pulse surge, that sense of excitement that always gripped her when she'd found the missing ingredient for one of her novels. Her delight spread to a grin as hot as the sun beating down on the roof of her Cherokee. It had taken seven long weeks, her deadline drawing near and her nerves churning with panic, but just as she'd decided all refurbished ghost towns were the same…voilà!

She dragged the brochure closer, then gazed out the windshield. Southern Montana spread beneath the pressing blue sky, the countryside ebbing away from the settlement in lazy rolling hills as far as the eye could see. The literature hadn't done it justice.

Alder Gulch was the exact image of the town she'd envisioned for the new story. There was no way she'd get everything she wanted in a week. She set the brochure on the seat beside her and shifted into gear, gently tapping the gas pedal. Would it be possible to stay longer, to write the bulk of the book here? The idea was tantalizing.

A nudge of guilt stole some of the idea's flavor. "You don't approve, do you, Gram?" She spoke aloud as if her grandmother were actually with her, as if she hadn't succumbed to the massive coronary she'd suffered two months ago. Gram had raised her, been her confidante, and somehow talking to her still seemed right and comforting. Besides, it was the only way she'd found to deal with the loss that lay heavy in her breast.

But Gram wouldn't approve of her being here. No, sirree! Gram would be livid. Andy frowned at the thought. Why had Gram spoken of Montana as if it were the Devil's Triangle? It was beautiful—the vast open spaces, the glorious mountains, the rivers, the prairies. It had it all. Including the friendliest residents she'd ever come across.

And the best part was, now she had a chance of meeting her deadline. Andy couldn't abide tardiness. Gram claimed she'd been impatience since birth, that she'd been born early, walked early and even talked early. Maybe. But she saw no reason for tardiness. A person merely needed organization and attention to detail—two assets Andy prided herself on possessing. Of course, Gram would add willfulness. Stubbornness. Disobedience.

Smirking, Andy maneuvered the Cherokee around parked cars and vans of all sizes and makes and pulled to a stop near a crowd of people gathered at the edges of the one main street bisecting Alder Gulch.

A college-aged man with a shock of white blond hair sticking out from under a dusty ten-gallon hat and a tin star pinned to his leather vest motioned for her to drive toward him and park beside the boardwalk, then he leaned toward her open window and stuck a flier at her. "Performance is about to start."

Andrea turned off the engine, then read the scrap of white paper with its bold blue lettering. Authentic Nineteenth-Century Melodramas—Performed Twice Daily By The Alder Gulch Players. It was as if she'd been expected. "You were wrong, Gram. Montana is welcoming me like a long-lost daughter. Not only have I found my town, I'm about to see a slice of life right out of one of my novels, in full-blown, living, breathing Technicolor."

Spectators hugged the sides of the streets, their expectant voices reflecting her own anticipation. Oh, yes. She'd been right to disobey Gram this time.

In a way it was Gram's own fault. *She* was the one who'd hidden, in her sewing box, the photograph of the mysterious man dressed like a gold miner. The moment Andy had come across it, she'd been fascinated. In fact, it had inspired the new book. But she had no idea who the man was, nor why Gram had kept the photograph a secret. And now there was no one to ask. She'd give anything to know if the man had been a relative. It was awful being all alone in the world.

Well, she wasn't exactly "all alone." Nor would she ignore everything Gram had wanted for her. "I might be the last of our line, Gram, but I'm a Hart through and through. I promise right after I finish this book, I'll marry Tim just the way you wanted, but I couldn't face planning the wedding without you. Not yet. So you'll just have to understand about the new book…and this trip."

She tugged off her sunglasses, wishing she could remove

her contacts for an hour or so, and shoved a strand of her dark brown hair toward the banana clip it had escaped. Her bare legs felt sticky against the leather seats now that the vehicle was motionless and the hot June air uncirculated.

Yanking a notepad and pen from the book bag always within reach on the seat beside her, Andy glanced down the street and began jotting descriptions of the blackened-wood buildings lining both sides of the dirt-packed road, the watering troughs, the wooden-railed boardwalks and the hitching posts with horses and wagons drawn up close. She was amazed at the great spot she'd managed to procure, given her late arrival. It had to be fate.

Her attention snagged on a strapping man, dressed all in black, as he broke through the bank doorway directly opposite her. The crowd quieted. A big Appaloosa waiting at a hitching post not five feet from the Cherokee let out a nervous nicker.

A gun blast exploded through her thoughts. Andy froze, her hand curling tighter around her pencil as she instinctively scrunched lower behind the steering wheel.

The man in black—whose gunfire had startled her—ran hell-bent across the street and leapt onto the Appaloosa, which looked sturdy enough to hold his magnificent proportions. He jerked the reins and spun the horse around, pulling up short inches from her front bumper.

In that moment their eyes met.

Andy felt as if an electrical shock had jolted through her. Here was the hero of her book. His hair was as black as polished onyx, his eyes the gray-green of sagebrush. She felt suddenly chilled—as if she were staring at the face of destiny. *Her destiny.* She doubted she'd ever seen a more handsome man...or one more deliciously dangerous looking.

"Stop him! He's stolen the orphans' fund!" Six or seven men, each brandishing either pistol or rifle, raced down the wooden sidewalk after the man in black, their gunfire punctuating their frantic pursuit.

Feeling as if she were watching a scene from the new novel being played out before her, Andy forgot to breathe. The man in black tipped his hat to her, then ducked low in the saddle.

Her heart raced like the group gaining on the thief.

More gunfire was exchanged, accompanied by fresh shouts and the hammering of boots on hard-packed earth.

The man in black yanked the reins and dug his bootheels into the horse's flanks. The Appaloosa sprang into action, lurched away from her Cherokee and galloped straight for the pursuing crowd. The stunned posse froze. The man in black let out a war whoop and, alternately firing both his silver pistols, scattered his pursuers and made a clean getaway down the street toward the end of town.

Applause erupted.

Grinning, Andy scooted erect in her seat and let out a miniature war whoop of her own. After seven weeks of searching, she'd finally found the right town and the right man.

The crowd quickly dispersed. Car doors opened and banged shut. She waited, letting those in a hurry to leave drive around her. Catching sight of the towheaded college student who'd handed her the flier, she stepped out of the Cherokee and got his attention. "Where might I find the outlaw?"

"Who, Black Jack?"

"I suppose…if that was him on the Appaloosa."

"It was." His smile showed even white teeth, and his deep blue eyes swept assessingly over her gauzy, long-sleeved peasant's blouse, across her shorts and down her long, tanned legs. It was obvious he liked what he saw. "Maybe I can help you instead? Cliff Mott's the name."

Indeed, Andy thought, recognizing the come-on for what it was. Yes, indeed. Montana was jam-packed with friendly people, but she doubted old Cliffie would take too kindly to her active imagination metamorphosing him into less than hero material. "I appreciate the offer, Mr. Mott, but I'm afraid only Black Jack will do for my purposes."

Cliff pressed his lips together, almost a pout. "Well, if you're certain…?"

Andy laughed. She'd never been more certain of anything. "Positive."

"In that case, you might try the hotel bar after the next performance an hour or so from now."

"Great. Thanks." An hour or so would give her time to check in to the motel, unpack, shower and change clothes.

Andy got back into the Cherokee and started the engine. She knew she was grinning like an idiot, but she didn't care. Her glee was irrepressible. "Hot damn, Gram! This is going to be one good book."

Horses and wagons now shared the street with automobiles and foot traffic. Andy drove slowly, half expecting to spot the assay office that was also pictured in her mysterious photograph. She knew it was a long shot, but considering all the magic that had been bestowed on her thus far this afternoon, why not one more miracle? Why not the icing on the cake?

Two tourists leapt into her path. Andy braked. As she waited for them to cross the street, she noticed she was abreast of the hotel. A delicious image of her impending meeting with Black Jack began to form in her head and her gaze lifted to the sign above the door. The Golden Broom Hotel. Andy's eyebrows twitched. What a different name. Was there an interesting story behind it? One she could use in her new book?

A sudden, unexpected chill swept through her, drawing goose bumps on her summer-warmed skin and stealing her smile. The eerie feeling was something akin to…to déjà vu. Oblivious to the horn honking behind her, Andy scanned the two-story building again. It was whitewashed and charming and impossibly familiar.

Impossibly.

She frowned, as if scowling would open her memory to anything she couldn't recall, like the car accident that had claimed the lives of her mother and father when she was five.

Everything including and preceding the accident was a complete blank. The doctor said she couldn't remember because it frightened her too badly. Dwelling on it still tightened her skull with terror. She didn't care if she never remembered. It wouldn't bring them back.

She forced her attention to the present, to the concerns of driving, and moved her foot to the gas pedal. Gram had done her best to fill the gaps. And they didn't include Montana. If she didn't know anything else, Andrea Eloise Hart knew she'd never been here. Gram had made certain of that.

The sense of familiarity persisted. Andy shook her head at herself. Of course she'd feel a twinge of déjà vu. After all, this was the seventh Western ghost town she'd visited in as many weeks. That was all it was.

Her destination—the Motherlode Motel—was at the far end of town. The sooner she got there and checked in, the sooner she could get to her interview with Black Jack. Andy shoved the long sleeves of her gauzy shirt up to her elbows. Sunlight fell across her left wrist, highlighting an old scar, three lines of raised, puckered skin that looked as if she'd once escaped the talons of a huge bird of prey.

Chapter Two

"Yer cabin's all ready," Mrs. Minna Kroft, the proprietress of the Motherlode Motel, informed Andy as soon as she'd introduced herself. "Even got the desk ya asked fer."

Minna's face was flat, with a hint of half-moon cheeks below slanted amber eyes, her hair a fluffy, flyaway gray. If Andy didn't know it was impossible, she'd think the woman and the big Persian cradled in her arm had the same ancestry.

She tapped the registry book. "Jest need yer Jane Doe."

As Andy reached for the pen, something warm and furry nuzzled her leg. She flinched, glanced sharply down and found herself looking into the fierce yellow eyes of a long-haired black cat with four white paws. Inexplicably a shiver scurried down her spine and a word spilled from her. "Boots…"

"Pardon?" Mrs. Kroft was reaching for the cabin key. She glanced over her shoulder. "You say somethin'?"

"No. It was nothing." Andy had no idea why she'd called the cat Boots, nor why her throat suddenly felt as if she'd swallowed a fur ball. But she could swear the room was shrinking. She quickly scrawled her name, then followed Mrs. Kroft outside.

"So, yer a writer?" She set the Persian on the porch, then led the way toward a knoll behind the motel office. "What kind of stuff do ya write, anyhow?"

"Historical romance novels, heavily laced with adventure." And steamy love scenes—created strictly from fantasy and for which she'd been both praised and condemned. If her critics only knew the limits of her experience! Andy shoved the thought away.

The sun was rapidly dipping out of sight, streaking the sky with long ribbons of pink and yellow, and a brisk breeze was blowing. Ahead were thirteen cabins that looked as though they'd been slapped together in the late 1800s and abandoned as soon as the gold strike in Alder Gulch ran dry.

Mrs. Kroft glanced over her shoulder. "Can't say I've ever heard of ya. But we've got us a real famous author lives right here in town."

Andy asked, "Who is that?"

"Goes by some bug's name, but he's really Eugene Mott. Likes to be called Gene."

Mott as in Cliff? But Andy could think of no "real famous" author named Mott. "The name doesn't ring any bells."

"Probably not, but ya wouldn't forget any of his stories. They're the kind that cause a body to keep the light on all night."

Behind the cabins, the prairie rolled into the distance as far as Andy could see, and at the moment the breeze was lifting dust and swirling it along the bleak knolls like miniature tornadoes. Mrs. Kroft startled her when she stopped abruptly and spun around. "Gypsy Moth! That's Gene's writing name."

Andy stopped in her tracks. Her mouth had dropped open. "Gypsy Moth, the queen of horror, is actually a man?"

"Yep." Mrs. Kroft chuckled. "Gene lets people think he's a woman 'cause he likes his privacy. Never goes on them talk shows or has his picture in any of his books."

Andy didn't think she'd put her photograph on her book jackets either if she wrote the kind of dark stories Gypsy— Gene Mott—wrote; however, it was interesting that he was living in Alder Gulch and that she'd probably met his relative—ole Cliffie. She might not care for Mott's stories, but she did respect his talent and maybe she could wangle an introduction before she left town.

Mrs. Kroft climbed the porch of the farthest cabin to the left and unlocked the door. Although there were clearly only thirteen cabins, Andy's bore the number fourteen. She stifled a grin and joined Mrs. Kroft on the porch.

The motel owner shoved the door inward, creating a gaping opening that looked as if it led to a black hole. Andy had a sudden sense of what her heroines had faced in the world before electricity. Wouldn't it be wonderful if she could write the novel, or most of it, in this cabin?

Tim would understand, probably even encourage the idea. After all, she had a deadline. Sometimes she wished he wouldn't be so blasted understanding.

Mrs. Kroft hit the light switch, chasing out the darkness and presenting the brightest pink walls Andy had ever seen.

"Pretty color, don'tcha think? Painted it myself."

"Cheery," Andy lied, thinking it ghastly. Paint had been slapped thickly on the walls as if someone were trying to cover a crime. However, she couldn't fault the clean look or smell of the place. Even Gram—a neat freak—would have approved.

The single room was twelve feet square with bathroom, kitchenette, dinette set and an iron-framed, antique bed. A hot-pink cloth draped a doorframe, obviously the closet, and a potbellied stove with a stack of chopped wood hugging its side claimed another corner. The linoleum floor—which might once have been red and black—was now pink and gray. Braided rugs attempted to cover its present humiliation.

"Hope this'll do." Mrs. Kroft hovered near a metal desk that stood beneath one of the room's three windows. "Furniture's scarce as hen's teeth 'round here. I was lucky ta come by it. Purely fate."

"Yes, fate," Andy agreed. Something had had a hand in her coming here, something beyond her own machinations. She could feel it in her bones. "It will do nicely."

A pleased smile crinkled the woman's feline features. "Well, if there ain't nothin' else—I'll let ya get settled."

"Oh, Mrs. Kroft, there is something. I passed a museum just up the road. Is it open for business during the day?"

Standing in the doorway, Mrs. Kroft nodded her head vigorously, causing her fluffy hair to wave like a detached hand. "Opens up every day 'round eleven. That and the library. Duke Plummer runs 'em. Been Plummers in Alder Gulch since the first gold strike. Anything ya wanna know about this town, Duke is yer man." She closed the door.

Alone in the ancient cabin, Andy took another stroll around the room, imagining the walls were as rustic as the outside suggested, that the floor was hard-packed dirt and the only light came from an oil lamp. With her eyes closed and her arms wrapped around her rib cage, she could almost smell the dirt, the lamp oil. The wind whining against the outer walls sweetened the images in her head.

Andy opened her eyes and spun around once. "Oh, Gram, I feel such a connection with Alder Gulch…as if I've lived here in another lifetime." Sadness crept into her voice and grabbed her heart. "I wish you were here to share it with me, Gram. I know Alder Gulch would have changed your mind about Montana."

Fearing she'd give in to the tears burning the back of her eyelids, Andy busied herself unpacking the Cherokee and her luggage and organizing the room to her liking.

In the bathroom she removed her tinted contacts and inspected herself in the mirror above the sink. Her oddly colored eyes—one blue, the other three-quarters brown and one-quarter blue—looked weary. Her hair was limp and dusty. She started the shower and, half an hour later, felt and looked a hundred percent better.

She brushed her shoulder-length, coffee brown hair off her face and contained it in a ribbon at her nape, then donned a short-sleeved sundress the exact blue of her tinted contact lenses. She placed a wide, hammered-silver bracelet over the scars on her left wrist, then checked the time. Unbidden anticipation rushed through her at the idea of seeing Black Jack again, of interviewing him.

She lifted her purse from the bed. The vision of the mysterious man in the photograph that was tucked within its depths flashed into her mind. She withdrew the sepia print. The man featured stood before an assay office…which was what had sparked the story idea of a heroine swept up with gold fever, willing to risk unimagined hardships to strike it rich and save her sisters and herself from a life of mortal sin.

The man's face was unfamiliar. Was he a relative? Or a stranger? There were no printer's marks, no studio name on it, but although it appeared old, the expert she'd consulted claimed it was taken in the late 1960s, or mid-1970s.

The man was dressed in the garb of a miner from the 1800s, but something about his shoulder-length hair, his ragged beard and his loose-limbed stance suggested his real wardrobe consisted of bell-bottom pants, tie-dyed T-shirts and headbands. But where had this picture been taken? Why had Gram hung on to it all these years? Hidden it in her sewing box?

"Who is he, Gram?" she asked aloud. The awful thing was, Andy had the prickling notion she ought to know.

She pulled open the cabin door. A black cat with white paws scurried off the porch, spooking her as thoroughly as she'd spooked it.

Ten minutes later, the spooky, spooked cat all but forgotten, Andy shoved through the swinging doors of the Golden Broom Hotel. The restaurant was packed, vibrating with the clink of silver and glass, the gabble of conversation, the occasional loud guffaw, the whine of a tired child and the unrelenting lilt of hurdy-gurdy music issuing from a player piano.

Seeking Black Jack, she swept her gaze over the dining room, over diners perched on rough-hewn wooden chairs pulled up to equally rustic-looking tables—indulging in various stages of the five-course meal offered as the evening fare—and over the slew of college-aged women who waited tables dressed as dance-hall girls of old in gaudy costumes and garish makeup with ostrich feathers in their hair.

Not finding him, she spun toward the bar and caught a whiff of stale cigarettes and whiskey, an odor prevalent in such establishments. A massive brass-and-mahogany antique bar consumed one entire wall. Behind it, huge mirrors hung on either side of an oil painting of an amply endowed nude reposing on pillows. Andy's pulse took an unexpected leap. *There he was...* below the nude...standing with his back to the bar, looking right at her.

JACK STARETT, JR., still wearing his Black Jack costume, propped his elbows on the bar behind him, hooked a bootheel on the brass footrest and arched his back against the aged mahogany. The beer he'd just downed had wiped the taste of dust and horse from his throat and was now working on the knot in his stomach.

Like the soft haze of cigarette smoke, his gaze floated through the dining room of the noisy Golden Broom Hotel until it came to rest on the woman framed in the wide doorway.

"Hey, pardner, checkin' out the fillies?"

Jack peered sideways at Cliff Mott. A lock of white blond hair dangled artistically over his forehead and his grin was lascivious, his gaze suggesting they were sharing a lewd joke. Jack knew plenty of men like Cliff—swinging bachelors, no strings, leery of roots and commitments. The exact opposite of everything Jack wanted for himself. "I'm just enjoying my beer. I'll leave the conquests to you."

"Hey, that's the pretty little piece I was talking to this afternoon. Now, there's a conquest you've already made."

Jack glanced again at the woman standing in the doorway. "You're nuts. I've never seen her before."

"Sure you have. This afternoon. You nearly rode the Appaloosa through her car grille."

It came back to him in a rush...the woman in the red Cherokee he'd tipped his hat to. He hadn't known why he'd done that or, for that matter, why he should recall her at all. Doing two shows a day, he paid little attention to the tourists; it was the residents of Alder Gulch who occupied his thoughts. But he did remember her.

BLACK JACK WAS even larger than she'd recalled...a great bear of a man. His hat was absent and his thick black hair was combed straight back off his high forehead, revealing a scowl as savage as that of a grizzly and giving him the look of a man with an attitude. A big bad attitude.

"What do you think, Gram? Isn't he perfect?"

She could almost hear Gram say, "Nobody's perfect, you foolish child."

Andy felt her first faltering hesitation and had to admit that on her way to the hotel she'd been wondering if she'd feel the way she had this afternoon about him. He might fit the role physically, but what if he was a mental dud, or worse, a nerd? She drew an unsteady breath as her gaze—starting at his dusty black leather boots and lifting slowly upward—caressed every lean, muscular inch of the gorgeous man.

"MAN, I'D LIKE TO BE in your Tony Lamas," Cliff said in a low aside to Jack.

The woman was beelining for them, and Jack had to admit she was easy on the eyes: at least five-seven, slender, yet curvaceous enough to hold his attention, especially in that long clinging blue dress. The way she moved, a graceful, long-limbed stride, spurred a vision of her in denims and boots, astride a restless stallion, a Stetson angled sexily atop her shiny brown hair, the brim grazing her sienna brows and accentuating her startlingly blue eyes.

Without looking away from her, he asked, "Are you sure it was me she wanted to see?"

"Yeah. I don't understand it, either. I offered her steak—" Cliff poked his own chest as though he were tapping a tender filet mignon. "But she said her tastes ran to chopped liver."

Before Jack could respond, the woman was there.

"Hello again," Andy said, stopping in front of Jack, but directing her gaze and her comment to Cliff.

"Evening. I was just telling our bandit here that you wanted a few words with him."

Andy felt Black Jack's assessing gaze whisking her like the fine strokes of a painter's brush. Her pulse skipped annoyingly. What was the matter with her? It was one thing to imagine herself in the nineteenth century and quite another to feel like some demure flower of the Old West whose propriety kept her from looking a man squarely in the face. Andy lifted her chin and smiled sweetly. "Actually, I'd like an interview."

"An interview?" Alarms went off in Jack's head. Was this fantasy-stirring little beauty a fellow reporter who was about to blow his cover sky-high?

Cliff said, "Well, I can see you two want to be alone, and my uncle is beckonin' me from over yonder."

Andy watched him cross to a table where one of the diners sat in a wheelchair, and she wondered fleetingly which of the men at the table was Eugene—Gene—Mott. But—as though his very aura were magnetic—her attention never fully left the man beside her. Oddly self-conscious, she extended her hand toward Black Jack's massive chest and gazed up into his sage green eyes. Her mouth was as dry as scorched grass. "My name is Andrea Hart."

Unusually disconcerted, Jack stared at her hand for a five-second beat, then reached for it. "Jack Sta...uh...Black. Jack Black." Her touch sent an electric current through him, but the heat in his face was for his faux pas. That was the first time he'd faltered over his alias. It had better be the last. Fortunately, no one was standing nearby, but he didn't want another misstep within the wrong earshot.

Jack's deep voice relieved Andy's earlier doubts; the unexpected tingle his touch caused both dismayed and pleased her. There was nothing dudish or nerdy about a man who made her this aware of her sexuality. Too aware of her sexuality. Oh, yes, he was A-one hero material.

But she was an engaged woman. This response to this man was wrong. She tried concentrating on her interview. On her story. The name Jack Black would never do. She'd have to come up with something better for her fictional hero.

Jack made no move to release her hand, which felt as warm and smooth as the underbelly of a calf in his big, callused one.

"Ooh, what's that in the tank?" Andrea's lovely face was scrunched in a grimace, her gaze focused on the small, rectangular glass tank that hugged one corner of the bar. An engraved sign warned: Dangerous. Do Not Touch.

"Scorpion. We have some native ones, but this fellow is particularly nasty—the deadliest of his species. Belongs to the owner of the hotel."

Although the yellow critter with two black stripes on its back huddled in one corner of the tank looking more shy than deadly, Andy shuddered. "Yuck."

Jack nodded, distracted by her mouth. It was puckered as if she were expecting a kiss. Unexpectedly, he wanted to oblige her. It took willpower to hold back. "Would you like a beer?"

"I'd love a beer."

He ordered two, then, taking her elbow, steered her toward a vacant table in a deserted corner. She had his male hormones working overtime and the skin at his nape prickling. Before he acted on his baser desires, he'd better figure out who she was and what she wanted from him. "Are you a reporter?"

"What? Oh, the request for an interview. No. I'm an author. I'm researching my latest novel, and you're very like the hero I have in mind."

She watched his ebony brows twitch, first in surprise, then in thought. He was either a methodical thinker or…slow. She fervently hoped for the former and decided methodical was a good trait for the hero in her book, especially if she could capture with words the essence of this Jack Black and the Jack Black already taking shape in her mind.

Hero? Jack grimaced. If he hadn't stuck so long to his belief that Nightmare Man was a random serial killer, Karen Bradley might still be alive. The thought filled him with a self-loathing that spilled over into his words. "I'm nobody's hero, lady."

Andy peered up at him. The man couldn't be more wrong. His brooding tone and self-deprecation—not to mention the erotic images he stirred in her—made him the perfect wounded hero for a romance novel. "I guess that depends on your description of hero. I don't expect you're as bad as the character you play, either."

"Don't count on it." Jack's grip tightened on his beer bottle. Being nice to the tourists was part of his job and some of the town council were in the dining room tonight, but having his attention diverted by the delectable Ms. Hart would get him no closer to finding his quarry.

"I promise my questions won't hurt."

He tugged on his beer, feeling the tightness in his forehead that meant he was scowling. He planned to mingle with the locals tonight, try to get a lead on which of them was the man he sought, and he couldn't do it until he got rid of this distracting author. "What do you want to know?"

Andy wanted to know why his voice sent shivers down her spine, why his cool, sage green eyes stirred something warm and disturbing deep inside her, why men who exuded his raw sexuality always inspired in her a desire to run as far and fast as she could. "I have a list here somewhere."

Pushing down her bothersome feelings, she fished in her purse and laid hold of the pen and tablet she sought. Why was it she had no problem fantasizing love scenes that made the pulse beat faster and the pleasure worth the risk? It wasn't as if she'd ever felt anything close. In her experience, sex was…disappointing. Somehow…unfulfilling.

But it sold books.

And every once in a while, like now, with this man, she had the sensation there might be something more to it than she'd ever known. Was ever likely to know. She stared into his seductive eyes and the yearning to know, to be taught by Jack, welled inside her. With her cheeks burning at the brazen thought, she flipped the tablet cover open to a clean page, set her list of questions to one side and readied the pen to write.

"I want to know everything you can tell me about horses and guns, all the smells, the sounds, the tastes, the touches, the slang. I've ridden horses, even shot a pistol, but I want a man's perspective."

"Sounds like a mighty tall order."

"We can go one question at a time."

Jack decided if he kept his responses short, the interview could be terminated in good speed.

Andy began, taking notes as he spoke, her nervousness forgotten as she wondered at the clipped, almost guarded edge to his intriguing voice. But before long she sensed his reticence waning.

Jack, impressed with her no-nonsense attitude, began to relax and slipped into answering the questions with an ease born of lifelong experience with the subject. But his mind was never far from his real concern and as he talked his gaze skipped about the room locating residents he now shared nodding acquaintance with—like Cliff's uncle, Gene Mott, a big-deal author in the horror genre. He was a cripple in a wheelchair with a meek demeanor who seemed to watch everyone and listen carefully to all that was said to him, sort of the way this Hart woman was doing with him. Authorese, he supposed.

Jack ordered them each another beer, then returned his concentration to Andrea. He was surprised how much he liked the way her mouth quirked as she asked questions; in fact, he liked her mouth a little too much. The urge to kiss her lips until they were swollen with passion swept through him.

He fought it down, concentrating instead on her other attributes, like her quick smile, her sudden laugh, the pride and confidence she exuded. She had a self-assuredness that the lucky had bred into them in childhood by loving encouragement and the solid foundation of family and roots.

He doubted Andrea Hart had a concern about who she was, where she'd been or where she was going. In other circumstances, they might have been friends. Desire teased him. Or more.

Again he shoved the thought away, stifled the urges. He wasn't in Alder Gulch looking for love. The beer seemed to sour in his stomach, leaving a bitter aftertaste on his tongue for all that his obsession had cost him. For her sake, he hoped nothing ever ripped away the roots of Andrea Hart's foundation as it had done to him.

"Do you spell Black the usual way?" she asked.

"Yes." Jack's slipping guard shot back into place like a spring-bolt lock. "Why does that matter? You don't need my name."

"Oh, but I do. I always include a section in my books for

thanking the people who contribute to the research, and your contribution—''

''I don't want my name in your book.''

Andy frowned. This was a first; she'd had several people insist their names be included in her books, but never before had anyone insisted they be excluded. *Gee, Gram, the man acts like he has something to hide.* ''Are you sure—''

''Dead certain.''

She dropped the subject. ''Could you tell me something about roping and branding cattle?''

Listening with half an ear, Andy wrote ''Sta'' next to Black on her tablet, adding a question mark beside it, then studied Jack with new interest. What hadn't she noticed about him before that should have registered as matter out of place?

It took a minute, but then she realized, for starters, there was his seemingly intimate knowledge of everyday ranch life. For another, his age. He was much older than most of the college students working in town. So probably he wasn't doing this for the fun of it. Yet if he were a professional actor it was more likely he'd spend these months doing legitimate summer stock.

Andy took notes, but her mind was on Jack. Throughout the interview—even now—his gaze wandered the room as if he were watching for someone or something.

Curiosity built to a force inside her, and as his attention swung back to her, she blurted out, ''Why is a man of your age and obvious good health wasting his time in a summer job that can't pay well and has no apparent benefits?''

Jack felt the warmth drain from his face. He gazed at her beneath lowered lids. Who the hell was this woman? It served him right for thinking nice thoughts about her. For wanting to kiss her. He couldn't trust anyone and he'd better not forget it. ''Now, how could knowing my personal business possibly help you with that book you're writing?''

What do you think, Gram? Did I strike a nerve? Andy

shrugged, but her pulse was racing, and she feared her expression might be smug. "You're very good at playing Black Jack, but I have a couple of friends who are actors and somehow I can't picture you doing that for a living."

Jack looked like a thundercloud about to spew lightning bolts.

Andy wasn't put off. She'd remembered something else. *He stuttered over his name. Yes, he did. And turned bright red over the fact.* She arched a brow and asked mockingly, "Who are you really, Jack, Sta—ah—Black?"

With a murmured curse, Jack scraped back his chair, rocking the table. Then, as quickly as a switched-off light, his expression softened. Andy watched the metamorphosis with suspicion. It was as if he'd become suddenly aware of where he was, of who might be watching. She curbed the urge to glance behind her.

He scooted the chair forward until his flat stomach grazed the table, then he plunked both elbows down and leaned toward her. Casual. Relaxed. Not a care in the world. A low chuckle slid from his sensuous mouth, and his eyes danced with mirth. "I'll bet you're one hell of a writer."

It was a good recovery, one that sent little shards of awareness through her and again aroused in her a desire to be kissed by this man. But it also convinced Andy she was right about him. Jack Black was not on the up-and-up. She raised one eyebrow and addressed his compliment. "And why is that?"

"'Cause you've a mighty large imagination, Ms. Hart."

There was no denying that—and Andy doubted he'd like the "what ifs" it was conjuring about him at the moment. "I guess you don't want to satisfy my curiosity?"

A low heat of desire danced in his sage green eyes. "Satisfying you would be my pleasure."

Andy's pulse wobbled.

A lazy grin tugged at Jack's sensuous mouth. "But there's no need for curiosity. The state of the national economy is no secret. I'm just a down-and-out cowboy, grateful as all get out to the Alder Gulch city council for giving me a roof over my head, food for my belly and beer to wash it down. Now…'' He stood abruptly, his sexy gaze still studying her face. "If you'll excuse me, I have to mingle.''

Feeling as though she'd just been mentally ravished, Andrea lurched to her feet. There was about Jack the sense of a wild stallion in a corralled pen, and it tugged at her curiosity, yanked at everything feminine in her. "Thank you for taking the time to answer my questions. If you change your mind about being included in the appreciation section of the book, you can find me at the Motherlode Motel.''

"I won't change my mind.'' Jack didn't tell her that he, too, was staying at the Motherlode, or that he'd try not to run into her again before she left town. He didn't want any further contact with this woman. She was too nosy, too good a judge of character, too easy to talk to, too easy on the eyes, too hard on the libido.

As she turned to gather her notebook and purse, she caught the edge of her bracelet on the chair. It flipped off her arm, flew against Jack's chest and clattered to the floor.

Reflexively, Jack retrieved it. She thanked him, her smile warming him as no other had in a very long time. Smiling back, he started to drop the bracelet into her outstretched palm, but the hunk of silver clung to his suddenly damp fingers when he noticed the scar on her wrist.

So help him, it looked like… The thought broke off. No way. It couldn't be.

He lifted his gaze to Andrea Hart's face. The startling blue of her eyes suddenly struck him as unnatural. Artificial. Could she be wearing colored contacts?

Could she have one brown eye and one blue eye? Despite the illogic, the million-to-one chance, hope sprouted. Could this be Leandra Woodworth? The bracelet bit into his palm.

No. He was thinking crazy. Mad. And yet, he couldn't convince himself that it was impossible.

He grasped her hand, fought to keep his grip gentle, and somehow managed to keep the emotion tearing through him out of his voice. "Looks like something mean tried taking a bite out of you. How'd it happen?"

Chapter Three

How had it happened? How had she gotten the scars on her wrist? Gram had said it happened the night her parents died, probably a piece of twisted car metal. That was all Andy ever needed or wanted to know about the scar. Pain centered behind her eyes, and she noted Jack's tanned face seemed rather ashen. Nonetheless, his touch was reassuring. "I was very young at the time. I can't—ah—don't remember."

Didn't or couldn't remember? Lee Lee Woodworth hadn't been able to remember anything but Nightmare Man. Jack cautioned himself against the excitement he felt stirring in his gut. "How young?"

Andy frowned. Why should he care how old she'd been? "Five or so."

Jack's pulse skipped, but he feared he was grasping at straws. So what if she'd received a scar on her left wrist the same as Lee Lee Woodworth, at about the same age? It proved nothing. Leandra's grandmother would never have allowed her to return to Alder Gulch without certain knowledge of who she was and what this town had meant to her. No, he was an idiot even to consider the notion, too damned anxious for an easy resolution to his own problem, a neat wrapping up of his years of searching.

"May I have my bracelet?"

"Oh...sure." Jack let go of her arm and handed over the

bracelet, which she promptly put back on, completely hiding the scar. The warmth of her hand in his lingered and with it a persistent, indefinable anxiety. Like worry. For her.

What was he concerned about? She looked nothing like Marcy Woodworth. And if Wally's theory held, that was the only thing that would put her in jeopardy. Unless... The urge to ask her if she was wearing colored contacts persisted, but Jack suspected that was the obsession working its head games, and suppressed the urge.

Hadn't he just been thinking how confident and self-assured she was? Would someone with Lee Lee's past be this self-possessed? No. She was not Leandra Woodworth. She was just a woman of about the right age, with a similar scar. A damned similar scar. His gaze landed on her mouth, and the instantaneous urge to kiss her jarred him again. Damn it. He'd already given her all the time he had to spare. "It's been... interesting, Ms. Hart. Take care."

Bemused at his abrupt departure, Andy watched him walk toward the table where Cliff had retreated. She'd have sworn he was dying to ask her something and, in truth, she had a few unanswered questions of her own—like why his curiosity about her scar seemed personal, like why she, an engaged woman, wanted to be kissed by him.

Jack Black was definitely a puzzle, and she loved a good puzzle. She settled her purse strap over her shoulder, glancing at him again, debating the propriety of following him.

JACK APPROACHED THE TABLE Cliff had gone to, not surprised to find that several of the locals had joined Cliff and his uncle. It was, he'd learned, a Saturday-night ritual. They made room for him, and Jack sank down next to Duke Plummer, curator of the local museum.

Plummer, a lodgepole pine of a man, claimed he was descended from the notorious outlaw, Henry Plummer, who'd once terrorized this area. He looked more like an old Harley-

Davidson man than a collector of town memorabilia, with his long, silvery black hair in a ponytail at his nape and his square jaw peppered with whiskers. His indigo eyes sparkled with devilry. He was the right age to be Nightmare Man.

In fact, with the exception of Cliff and himself, so were all the men at this table, including Gene Mott. Gene was seated on his left in an electric wheelchair, puffing smoke from a Havana cigar toward the open rafters overhead. After some discreet inquiries, Jack had learned Gene's spinal injury was the result of a fall from a horse twenty or so years back. "Evening, Gene."

"Jack." Mott's voice was frail, belying his physical strength, his upper body was as well muscled as Jack's own.

"That babe a reporter?" Cliff asked.

"I'm an author," Andy answered from behind him.

Jack started, displeased at seeing her here. She gave him an innocent smile, but before he could respond, the man next to Gene Mott sprang to his feet, a show of manners, Jack noted, that was not extended by any of the other men at the table, himself included.

"Red Yager, owner of this humble establishment, ma'am." Red's shaggy head of hair and barbershop-quartet mustache were the color of rusted barbed wire, and his constant squint made Jack wonder if he needed glasses. Red pulled up a chair for Andrea. "Please join us."

"I don't want to intrude."

"Nonsense," Red gushed. "This table could use a little sugar. Sit, sit."

Andy took the seat opposite Jack, who handled introductions.

Red said, "Well, Gene. Another author in our midst. At least this one is easy on the eyes."

"Don't tell me." Cliff eyed her with a lustful glint. "Romance, right?"

"Historical romance, to be accurate." Andrea's tone told

Jack she took her occupation seriously, and he liked the way it silenced Cliff.

Red said, "Well, if history's your game, you should see Gene's personal library. Contains an incredible collection of diaries written during the cowboy and gold-mining eras of this town—including the time of Duke's infamous ancestor."

"Actual diaries written by former Alder Gulch residents?" Andy's heart beat faster, and she couldn't help looking expectantly at Gene Mott, hoping for an invitation to peruse the books.

Gene Mott ignored her, puffed his cigar and sipped his whiskey. Like the white female of the moth he'd taken his pseudonym from, he was as pale as an albino, with white-white hair, eyes the faded blue of a winter moon and skin as bloodless as a corpse. Indeed, he looked as gruesome as a character from one of his novels; probably the real reason he didn't like his photograph on his book jackets.

Determined not to be put off by his rudeness, Andy tried another tactic. "I greatly respect your work, Mr. Mott. Although I was disconcerted when Mrs. Kroft told me this afternoon that you were not a woman. I assumed—"

He turned his icy eyes on her then. "It is my intention that all should assume."

Duke Plummer coughed behind his hand. "I can help you with whatever history you need to know. Come see me at the museum—if you're going to be in town long enough."

"Oh, I'll be here long enough." Grateful for the curator's graciousness, Andy sat straighter in the wooden chair and smiled at him. "I intend to stay at least all summer."

Jack clamped his teeth together so hard he bit the inside of his cheek and winced. The dining room crowd was thinning, and the noise level was lower, but the hurdy-gurdy beat of the player piano seemed to drum a tattoo of the unnamed anxiety he felt for this woman. Hell, he'd known her less than an hour and already she'd gotten under his skin, as though they'd connected on some intangible, yet concrete, level.

Okay. It was part sexual, but that didn't explain the anxiety tremoring his gut. Damn. She could not, would not be his concern. But every protective instinct he had said otherwise. As long as she was in Alder Gulch, he knew he would feel the need to keep a close eye on her.

A waitress arrived at the table and as she took orders, Red asked, "What will you have, Ms. Hart?"

"Nothing, thanks." Andy didn't know whether it was the two beers or Jack Black's scrutiny causing the flutters in her stomach. "I haven't had dinner yet."

Red squinted at her, his mustache twitching. "Well, that settles it, then. Bring Ms. Hart tonight's special."

Andy protested to no avail, and when the country fried steak and mashed potatoes arrived, she was glad Red had prevailed. For the next half hour, while she ate and after, over a cup of black coffee, she answered the men's questions about her new book and her writing.

Gene Mott showed utter indifference, asking her nothing, offering neither opinion nor assistance. He looked as if the whole conversation bored him, which Andy realized it probably did. *After all, he's "been there, done that."* She sighed inwardly. He was going to be a tough nut to crack, but somehow, she would find the right hammer—anything to see those diaries.

Jack Black also abstained from comment, but although she'd felt his heady gaze on her more than once, mostly he seemed intent on studying one or another of the men at the table.

What is he looking for? He chose that moment to glance her way and as their eyes met, she felt something like an electrical charge pass between them, something she hadn't experienced before, something that bred goose bumps across every inch of her. Sexual awareness? Was this that wonderful sensation she wrote about like a well-schooled expert, but had never felt?

No. It couldn't be. *Don't worry, Gram, I'm going to marry Tim—not some brute of a cowboy-actor who isn't even certain what his name is.* She thanked Red Yager for the meal that he insisted was his treat, and stood. "I can't think of an evening I've enjoyed more, gentlemen, but I like to work first thing in the morning, so I'm going to call it a night."

Except for Gene Mott, the men all stood this time, their "good-nights" colliding.

Andy had just reached the door when Jack caught up to her. He had found his Stetson and was now wearing it. "Mind if I walk with you?"

Wishing her pulse would quit its crazy jig, she peered up into his sage green eyes. What she saw there only perplexed her more. If she didn't know better, she'd swear, beneath his disturbing interest, he was concerned about her welfare. But that was too absurd to be true; there was nothing for her to fear in Alder Gulch. "I wouldn't want to take you out of your way."

"You won't. I'm staying at the Motherlode, too."

"Oh, really."

Jack looked sheepish. "Guess I should have mentioned it earlier."

But Andy knew why he hadn't. After their interview he'd made it clear that he wanted nothing more to do with her. She followed him outside onto the boardwalk. What had changed his mind? Why was he all of a sudden offering her an escort to her cabin as if she were in dire need of a protector? Andy curled the fingers of her right hand over her left wrist and fought off the disquiet winding through her.

Main Street was deserted, shops and businesses closed for the night, tourists retired. The noise and music of the restaurant had lost the lively, inviting bounce of earlier. She fell in step with Jack. Except for the unsettling sensuality, she had to admit, she did feel safe in his company. It was as if he were a safe harbor in stormy seas, but Andy wasn't sailing through stormy seas, and wondered at the analogy.

Of course, she couldn't deny that since she'd arrived in town, one or two things had unsettled her, like calling a cat she'd never before laid eyes on ''Boots,'' and that weird sense of déjà vu. As though it were painted in glow-in-the-dark lettering the hotel's sign drew her attention. She stopped.

''What is it?'' Jack asked softly.

''Nothing.'' Andy shook herself and forced a smile. ''I just forgot to ask Mr. Yager how the hotel came to be called the Golden Broom.''

Jack shoved his hat off his forehead. The lazy smile was back, along with the seductive gleam in his eyes. ''I probably won't relate it as colorfully as Red, but I can give you the highlights.''

Andy stared at his mouth. ''Please do.''

''Okay. In the early 1900s, Alder Gulch was a thriving community.'' Jack caught her arm and they started moving again. ''The Conrey Placer Mining Company set up base in the area and remained here until the end of the dredging days, about 1923.''

Andy considered digging her tablet out of her purse and writing this down. It could certainly be used in her new novel. She glanced up at Jack, liking the way the evening lights reflected off the deep planes of his handsome face as he spoke. If she left the tablet where it was, she'd be able to ask him to repeat this story for her later. The thought brought a warm heat to her face.

''The largest dredge boat in the world at that time, Conrey's number four, worked this area between 1911 and 1922, and it's said they took twenty-two tons of gold out of the gulch.''

''Whew.'' But Andy said nothing more; instead, she listened, liking the deep baritone of Jack's voice.

''The old mining camp grew from a cluster of cabins to a

prosperous town when the dredges came in, and declined just as fast when they went out. But in the early days, when the town was booming, the sweeping of a saloon was offered for sale to the highest bidder. The story goes that once the chore was bid in for twelve dollars and netted the sweeper sixty-four dollars in gold dust. That was a lot of money in those days."

"Ooh. What a wonderful story." Andy laughed softly. "It's perfect for my novel."

"And it really happened." Jack liked the gentle way her laugh stroked his nerve endings, liked the feeling a lot. The urge to kiss her swept him again. Again he shoved it away. He must not allow himself to be distracted by her. His business in this town was too serious.

They'd reached the last shop at the end of the boardwalk. Andy's gaze drifted to the display window and once again she stopped and stared. It was full of sepia photographs like the one she'd found in her grandmother's sewing box.

Cupping her hands around her eyes, she perused the pictures of people wearing Old West garments. Hairstyles told her these were photographs of 1990s folk, but the backgrounds of the photographs were like something out of "Gunsmoke" or "Bonanza."

"Look like people out of your novels, do they?"

She glanced up at Jack. "Yes."

"Tourists. They love this place—dressing up like their ancestors and having their pictures taken in front of a backdrop that looks like an old livery stable or saloon."

Or assay office. Andy's pulse surged. Had her secret photograph been taken in a shop like this?

The door of the shop wrenched open and a man stepped out. "Something I can help you folks with?"

The man had faded brown air, permed in a style reminiscent of Mike Brady of "The Brady Bunch," and perched on his hawkish nose were John Lennon glasses that made his black eyes look even more round than nature intended.

He, also, Jack mused, was the right age to be Nightmare Man. Reflexively, he stepped between the man and Andrea, and tipped his hat. "Just window-shopping, Mr. Cooper."

"Oh, Black Jack Black. I didn't recognize you for a second there. Please, don't be so formal. Name's Virgil, but most call me Coop. I'll answer to either."

"Sure," Jack said. "Coop."

"If you're here about your proofs, Jack, they aren't ready yet." Coop locked the door to the shop, then dropped the key in his pocket. "Maybe tomorrow. Been inundated with tourists, you know."

"I'm in no hurry for them," Jack said.

"You had your picture taken here?" Andy asked Jack.

"Yep." Jack tugged the hem of his vest, indicating the outfit he wore now—the same outfit from this afternoon's performance. "For the City Players posters."

Coop removed his glasses and polished the lenses on a crisp hankie he'd withdrawn from an inside pocket of his jacket. He blinked at her. "You an actor, too?"

"No, not me." Andy decided she'd leave it at that. For now. But she intended to visit this shop tomorrow. With luck, she'd find some answers about her secret photograph, maybe even acquire a picture of Black Jack. "I'm just another tourist."

"Tourists are this town's bread and butter." Coop smiled and plunked his glasses back on his sharp nose. "Good evening to you both, then."

He stepped off the boardwalk and started up a side street, one of many that led to the hundred or so houses on the hillside behind town. Like teenagers on a date, Jack guided Andy across the street and down the lane that led to the motel. Wind rippled through the cottonwood trees, riffling the underbrush. Crickets chirped. The stars pressed down on them, and the air smelled rich and sweet. Andy thought it was a perfect night.

The path narrowed and she moved ahead of Jack to walk single file. The underbrush shuddered. Andy started. Jack grasped her by the shoulders. Her breath sucked in and her heart hitched. She thought for sure there must be a rattlesnake in her path.

But it was only a cat. Not the one with the white paws; this cat was all black. But Andy's every concentration was on Jack, on his heart thudding against her shoulder blades, on her own heart quickening to a similar rhythm, on his hot breath fanning her neck.

As if it were the most natural thing in the world, he pulled her around and into his arms. A second later he was kissing her, tentatively, then with a confidence she felt certain she was encouraging. Her insides had melted, puddling like heated chocolate, sweet and thick and good.

As blood rushed through his loins, creating a hard and solid ache, Jack jolted with the awareness of what he was doing, what he wanted to do. He pulled away from Andy. Only sheer strength of will kept him from kissing her inviting mouth again, but he knew if he did, he wouldn't quit with a few kisses. "We'd better get going."

Andy didn't know whether to feel ashamed for Tim's sake that she had so enjoyed the kiss, or to feel embarrassed because Jack seemed so sorry he'd initiated it. She turned away, took a step forward, then stopped.

Jack, shaken by the kiss and the desire still racking his body, wanted nothing more at the moment than to get her safely delivered to her cabin and go take a cold shower. He urged her on, but Andy didn't move. "What's the holdup?"

"Look for yourself." She scooted aside so he could see.

A big black cat with yellow eyes and a stub tail sprawled across the narrow path. It eyed him indolently, then continued washing itself. Jack frowned, his already accelerated pulse beating faster. Could this be Karen Bradley's cat, the unaccounted-for Outlaw? Hell, the odds against it were phenomenal, but it fit Wally Lester's description to a T. "Outlaw?"

Jack ignored the puzzled look Andy shot him. The cat stopped washing. He could tell it was poised for escape. "Outlaw?"

The cat fled down the path.

Leaving Andy staring after him, Jack chased the cat. It scooted ahead, then disappeared under the porch of the motel office. Jack knelt down. The odor of cat urine mingled with dry dirt. Wriggling his nose, he called, "Here kitty, kitty, kitty."

"Which cat ya lookin' fer?" Minna Kroft appeared from the shadows of the motel office.

Jack started. Slowly he straightened and faced the motel owner. It occurred to him in a sudden flash that Nightmare Man might actually be a woman. After all, Leandra Woodworth was a frightened child when she'd identified her parents' slayer. She could easily have mistaken this unfeminine creature for a man. Minna Kroft *was* the right age. His neck prickled. Had she heard him call the cat Outlaw? Andy was now watching him, too, waiting for an explanation of his odd behavior. He didn't look at her. "I don't know which cat. Black with yellow eyes, no tail. Seemed a mite skittish. I thought maybe it was ailing."

Jack was well aware that Andrea could call him on the lie. He held his breath, hoping she wouldn't.

Mrs. Kroft didn't give her a chance. "Ah, Satan. Sick, ya say? I hope yer wrong. He's purebred Manx."

Jack shrugged. "One cat looks pretty much like another to me."

"Phooey!" Mrs. Kroft gave a derisive snort. "Ya can't mistake one cat fer another—lest yer ignorant."

Or used to barn cats with indiscriminate breeding habits,

Jack mused. He nodded toward the porch. "Afraid I frightened him away."

"He won't wander far."

When they were alone again, a few yards from her cabin, Andy asked Jack, "What was that all about with the cat?"

But Jack, usually so quick on his mental feet, couldn't find the lie when he needed it, and he could hardly say, "I thought the cat might belong to a young woman who was murdered last autumn." He said, "Believe me, you don't want to know."

Andy gritted her teeth. He couldn't be more wrong. After the kiss they had shared, she wanted to know everything about Jack. Starting with his motives. As in her books, motives were everything. But if he wouldn't tell her his, then she would find some other way of discovering them. She already had a few clues to go on.

IN THE QUIET of his own home, Nightmare Man moved with purpose to the built-in bookcases. The mahogany shelves smelled of lemon oil, a fragrance he associated with cleanliness. But tonight he hardly noticed it. Worry held his attention.

He depressed the button that triggered the secret panel. Since his first encounter with Jack Black two weeks ago, he'd tried figuring out why the cowboy seemed familiar. Then all of a sudden this evening, he'd had an idea. He drew the photo album out of its hiding place, carried it to his favorite chair and sat in the glow of the reedy table lamp.

Stale paper smell rose from the book as he opened it and began flipping pages. Near the middle of the album he found what he sought: a yellowed, twenty-year-old newspaper clipping, flaunting the photograph of the reporter who'd written the story of the Woodworths' deaths.

Jack Starett, Sr.

The name brought bile rushing into his throat. It tasted bit-

ter on his tongue. Thrusting the photograph directly under the
lamp, he leaned closer, studying the man's features. He was
amazed at the depth of his hatred for the man so long de-
ceased.

Jack Starett, Sr., should have told him the whereabouts of
Lee Lee Woodworth. Instead, he'd pretended not to know,
and the headache had come like a tornado, dark and uncon-
trollable, and when it had finally gone, Starett had lain dead
at his feet. His life force pumping from the three gashes in
his throat.

He hadn't meant to hurt Starett. He hadn't meant to hurt
any of them. But they'd all made him so angry. He massaged
his temples. It was the headaches. As long as he stayed calm
and didn't get angry, he could control them.

He gazed down at the black-and-white newspaper photograph that smelled musty with age. Fear crawled through his
belly. Jack Black could be but one man: Starett's son, his
namesake, the man who'd chased like a bloodhound after
Nightmare Man's scent for the past fifteen years. Junior had
never come this close before.

He felt the anger stir anew, and closed his eyes until he'd
willed it to dormancy. All these years he'd moved freely in
this town, in this county, without worry of condemnation. Or
prosecution.

Should he be worried now?

No. Worry would bring on a headache. But if he stayed
calm, all would be fine. There was nothing here to link him
to the Woodworths' deaths. Nothing here to link him to Nightmare Man.

*But what is Starett's son doing in Alder Gulch, if not to
find me?* Despite his resolve, a tiny ache tweaked his temples.

Chapter Four

What's the matter with me, Gram? Thoughts of Tim never intrude on my work. Giving up in frustration, Andy stacked the character charts for the new book in a neat pile on the desk and stood.

All finished. Except for the hero's chart. Every time she'd started working on his, she'd been assailed with memories of Jack's kiss, and all the sensations that had sprung to life then had stirred anew. Again and again she set the chart aside, and when she thought she could control the wayward images and her dangerous responses to them, she'd try again.

But the moment she looked at the hero's name scrawled across the top of the page, Jack's face leapt into her mind, and her lips tingled as though his mouth had just left hers.

It was no use. Maybe later. With her sepia photograph tucked in her purse, she stepped out into the warm afternoon.

Mrs. Kroft was watering the sparse flower beds bordering the motel office. Andy caught sight of someone walking away from her. From the back it looked like Cliff Mott. She wondered fleetingly what business Cliff would have with Mrs. Kroft, and hoped it had nothing to do with her. As he disappeared down the path, her attention returned to the motel owner. She hadn't noticed before how tall the woman was or how much she was built like a man from the back.

Mrs. Kroft's feline features curled in a grin as she pivoted toward Andy, swinging the hose with her. "Ain't you a breath o' sunshine today."

Water splashed against Andy's sandal-clad feet, shocking yet pleasingly cool. She smoothed the cotton of her sleeveless sundress. "Thank you, Mrs. Kroft."

"Minna, child, Minna. It's so much friendlier."

"Okay, Minna. As long as you'll call me Andy." She smiled, deciding she liked being on a first-name basis with another woman, not bothered by their age differences as some might have been. After all, until two months ago, Gram had been her main confidante.

Without warning, the white-pawed cat leapt off the porch railing at her. Andy threw her hands in front of her face and leapt back. The cat bounded past her and scooted into the underbrush.

"Land sakes!" Minna exclaimed, alarm etched in her amber eyes. "The cat do that?"

Shaken, it took Andy a moment to realize Minna meant the scar on her left wrist. She lowered her hand, staring at it. "No. That happened when I was a child."

Minna stepped closer, her gaze riveted on the scar. Andy had the distinct impression Minna was going to grasp her wrist. Self-conscious, she turned her hand palm down and pressed it against her skirt, hiding the scar.

Minna blinked at her. Andy was suddenly uncomfortable and turned to leave. The offending cat darted out of the underbrush and came rushing at her again as if it were going to attack.

"Shoo!" Minna admonished, flicking the hose water at the cat. "Quit botherin' Andy."

It bolted away and Andy shot Minna a nervous smile. She couldn't imagine why the cat seemed bothered by her, or why she was bothered by it. Her throat constricted and an ache twinged her temples. "Guess he doesn't like me."

"Cats is funny." Minna sighed. "Never know who or what they's about."

Andy nodded, then turned toward the lane into town. Sort of like Jack Black. She didn't know who or what he was about, either. Arriving at the spot where he'd kissed her the night before, she tightened her grip on her purse strap and quickened her steps. She would not waste one more second on Jack Black.

A burst of gunfire brought her up short. The City Players were performing. Despite her best efforts to the contrary, Jack's image filled her mind and she realized if she kept on at this pace, she might well run into him.

But she needn't have worried. By the time she arrived on Main Street, tourists crowded the road. The performance was over. Despite all her denials, her heart beat faster at the possibility of seeing Jack and sank a little when he was nowhere in sight.

Cursing the man's effect on her, she entered the photography studio. It smelled of musty clothing and vanilla incense. Virgil "Coop" Cooper was busy posing a family of four dressed in costumes from the last century.

Behind them was the backdrop of a jail cell. It hung from the ceiling on some kind of retractable device, much like a projection screen. There were five such retractable devices, each, she assumed, depicting a different background.

The whir of the camera dragged her attention to the photographer. His white shirtsleeves were shoved to the elbows, held in place by wine red garters, and a thin black tie circled his neck, bringing to mind Hollywood versions of Brett Maverick. But Coop, with his permed, faded brown, seventies hair and John Lennon glasses, looked more like a bookworm than anyone's leading man.

He cocked his head and called out, "Be right with you."

"Sure." It struck Andy that her time might be better spent at the museum. She turned for the door and noticed three wooden barrels near the display window; each held different-sized prints like oversized postcards depicting various sites around town.

She browsed through them, paying little attention to the people in the photos; it was the backgrounds that interested her. However, by the time the family had departed, she'd gone through two of the three barrels and selected a few prints for future reference in conjunction with her book, without finding anything close to the assay office in her sepia.

"Well, now." Coop startled her. His black eyes looked as round as cue balls behind his funky glasses, but if he recognized her from the night before, he didn't show it. "What can I do for you?"

Andy gestured at the backdrops. "What else besides the jail cell do you have?"

"Looking for anything in particular?" Coop stepped around the camera and caught hold of the bottom of the jail-cell scene. With a snap it retracted into the ceiling mechanism.

"I don't suppose you have an assay office?"

He pushed his glasses up the bridge of his nose. "Actually, I do."

Andy held her breath.

"Not much call for it lately. Most people choose the sheriff's office or the hotel or the bar." He hooked a finger in the metal loop of the retractable backdrop nearest the wall. As the screen settled into place, he stepped away. "How's that?"

It was not the same as the one in her photo. Not even close. She ought to just show him her photograph and see if he could help. She reached into her purse, but as her fingers grazed the sepia, she had the oddest sense that she shouldn't show it to this man.

Frowning, Andy let out the breath paining her chest, withdrew her hand from her purse and shook her head at Coop, gesturing with her wrists outward. "Interesting, but not quite what I had in mind."

Coop's gaze settled on her scarred wrist. Had his pale face grown paler, or had she imagined it? As he opened his mouth to ask her what she was sure were the hated but inevitable questions, she thrust at him the prints she'd selected. "How much do I owe you for these?"

After her encounter with Minna and the cat, she didn't want to think about the ugly scar, much less talk about it. Why hadn't she worn her bracelet? Coop was handing her change when the door behind her opened. Heavy-heeled boots clumped into the shop and Andy felt eyes on her.

"Ain't this our lucky day? Afternoon, Ms. Hart."

Cliffie.

Andy spun around, ready to put him in his place. Jack was right behind Cliff, shutting the door. Her heart hitched and the wisecrack died on her tongue. Of its own volition, her gaze slipped over Cliff to Jack.

A smile flickered at the corners of his wonderful mouth, but his brows gave every indication of being permanently dipped in a scowl. *Gram, why am I so attracted to this man?*

Jack yanked his hat off his head, held it in front of him like a bashful little boy and nodded at her. "Andy."

Her pulse skittered and an annoying heat grazed her cheeks. "Jack. Cliff. How's it going?"

Coop interrupted. "Sorry about this. I got hold of a bad batch of film and wouldn't you know it would be the one I used to shoot the individual photos of the players."

"You'll probably be all week redoing 'em," Cliff laughed.

Coop blinked at him, but let the insult go unanswered. "Let's start with you, Black Jack. Just make yourself comfortable."

Jack brushed dust from his hat with the sleeve of his black shirt, ran his long fingers through his hair, then with an ease and confidence of practice years old, angled the hat on his head. The scowl tugging his brows over his sage green eyes added a dimension of sexiness Andy would swear he had no idea he exuded.

No longer anxious to leave, she busied herself inspecting the third barrel of prints, but her attention was focused on the photo shoot behind her. Absently she thumbed the prints—nearly identical to those she'd already purchased—hardly noticing what she was seeing. Something registered a microsecond after she'd passed it. Her hand stayed. Had she seen what she thought she'd seen?

Shakily she pushed the prints backward, then stopped. An odd thrumming in her ears wiped out the sounds of the men behind her. The print was of a couple standing in front of an assay office.

Her assay office.

Excitement swept Andy like a prairie fire. She snatched the print from the barrel. "Coop, where was this taken?"

She felt the men's eyes on her, especially Jack's. He seemed to be straining to see what she held. Coop's black eyes narrowed behind his round glasses. "Should say on the back. I buy those prints from a wholesaler. For all I know he gets them from Taiwan."

Andy's exhilaration lost its edge. Was that all her sepia photograph was—something someone in Taiwan had created? She turned the print over. Stamped on the back was the name and address of the photographer, a Montana company in a town only sixty miles away. At last, a clue. New hope sprang up in her. "Coop, I'm exchanging this print with one of the same price that I've already bought."

"Be my guest." Coop lowered his head to his camera. "Jack, look at me, not her."

Finally she had a name to call, someone who could tell her when this scene was photographed. And more important, where. Bubbling with purpose, she waved goodbye to Jack and left him scowling at Coop.

Andy hurried along the boardwalk, oblivious to the tourists

she crowded past. Coming to twin, oval-windowed doors, the entrance to the lobby of the Golden Broom Hotel, she grew thoughtful, her pace slowing until she came to the swinging bar door, where she stopped altogether. Recalling Jack's story, she realized he'd said the "original bar." Did that mean the hotel hadn't always looked as it did now? She pivoted and glanced the length of the building.

The bar doors swung open, almost slamming into her.

Andy jumped back.

Red Yager, looking alarmed at the near collision, exclaimed, "Whoa. Are you all right?"

"Fine. Just thinking."

"About your book—something I can help you with?" His generous rust-colored mustache twitched as he spoke.

She tilted her head. "You've probably got some old photographs of Alder Gulch."

"You betcha." Red squinted at her. "Got some fine ones of the gold rush days. Should be dandy for your book."

"Well, I was thinking about something a little more recent, say twenty or thirty years back."

"Twenty or thirty—" He squinted at her. "Can't be for your book. Why are you interested in that period?"

Reflexively, Andy reached inside her purse for the sepia, but as her fingers grazed it, she noticed Red staring at her scarred wrist with the strangest look in his eyes. She withdrew her hand, turning it palm down. His gaze lifted slowly to her face and there was a troubled expression in his eyes. She said, "Just call me curious."

"You know what they say about curiosity." Red laughed, but it was not a warm sound. "Sorry, I can't help you."

Couldn't or wouldn't help? Andy wondered. "Well, thanks, anyway."

What did it matter? she decided, moving along the boardwalk at a brisk pace. If she couldn't find what she wanted at the museum, she'd call the photographer whose name and studio were printed on the back of the glossy she'd bought.

The museum was two stories, constructed of cut sandstone, a drab beige the same color as the dusty street. Its narrow windows sorely needed washing.

Inside the light was murky, and myriad glass display cases sported fingerprints, many of them child-sized and smeary. She signed the guest register, then spun toward Duke Plummer, who sat at an antique table near one of the windows, clipping something from a newspaper.

His silvery black hair was banded at the nape with a leather thong. Laying his scissors aside, he glanced up as she approached. A smile slid across his rugged face. "Well, now, Ms. Hart. Ready for some history research?"

"Yes, actually. And I was hoping you could help."

"Be glad to try. Inherited my knowledge of this town and my job from my folks." He showed yellowed teeth as he spoke. "If it happened here, I can probably tell you about it."

"I'm interested in seeing what Alder Gulch looked like twenty or so years ago."

Duke's scruffy eyebrows lifted. "I thought your book was set in the 1860s?"

Andy's stomach tensed. "It is. But I was also interested in some of the newer history."

He let out a noisy breath, eyed her curiously, then grew thoughtful. "I've got a few photo albums of the last century and the early years of this century on display upstairs, but twenty years back...hmm."

As Andy waited she noticed that the something Duke Plummer was clipping from the newspaper was an article about the City Players. He probably had more memorabilia stashed around here than he could remember. She ought to just show him *her* photograph and see if he knew anything about it. Her hand delved into her purse.

"Wait a minute." Plummer lumbered to his feet. "My sister keeps the family album around here somewhere. Maybe that'll help.'' He went into the back room. Several minutes passed before he returned carrying an album as dusty as the outside of the building. He shoved his clippings and newspaper to one side, pulled up a seat for Andy, then plopped himself back into his chair. "Let's see what we've got.''

An anxious feathering, like so many frantic butterflies fluttered inside Andy's stomach as Duke opened the album. Poorly focused snapshots in brilliant Kodak color were plunked helter-skelter on the pages. Beneath each someone had scrawled names—presumably Plummer family friends or relatives—and dates.

"The town has had several face-lifts over the years." Duke's breath smelled of chewing tobacco, and Andy realized such a habit would explain his yellowed teeth. He pointed at the pictures. "Here's Boot Hill. And this is Main Street, right near the hotel.''

"Oh, my God!'' Andy reached out and stopped him from turning the next page. The anxious feathering in her stomach became a frenzied beating as what she was seeing registered. Several snapshots exhibited the same view. Her assay office was once part of the Golden Broom Hotel.

"What is it, Ms. Hart? Are you ill?''

"No. I'm fine.'' Confused, dumbfounded, but fine. This was getting more curious at each turn. Had Gram known someone in Alder Gulch? Had her hatred of Montana been based on personal experience? This time she did dig the sepia print from her purse. "Would you perhaps know this man?''

Plummer held the photograph at arm's length, peering down his nose at it for several seconds. Suddenly he tensed. His gaze—wide-eyed and leery, all friendliness gone—jerked to Andy and he shoved the sepia into her hand as if it had burned him. "Never saw the guy. Never.''

Shaking his head, he snapped the photo album shut.

"But—''

"I have work to do." He cut her off. "You're welcome to look around the museum."

Slowly Andy rose and tucked her sepia print back into her purse. Duke Plummer knew something—if not the man in her photograph, then something about him. Andy stifled her frustration. Prying anything out of him now would be impossible.

She left him clipping newspaper articles, wandered into the next room and inspected items in the glass cases and those hanging on the walls. In a corner she came upon four ancient-looking books.

Andy scanned them, but her heart wasn't on her task. She couldn't get the sepia photograph off her mind, couldn't stop wondering who the man was or why Gram had kept it hidden. As though just thinking about someone could conjure up their image, Andy realized she was staring at a likeness of her grandmother.

Shock rocked through her. The photograph was of three women standing outside a tent. No! It was impossible. At the time this photograph was taken Gram would have been a baby. Andy's hands trembled. The book wavered unsteadily.

She read the names listed below the picture, finding the one for the woman who looked like her grandmother. Enid Leach. Andy's heart lurched and her mouth dried. Gram's mother's name was Enid Leach.

Reeling as if the very core of her existence were slipping from beneath her, Andy somehow managed to set the book back on the table. Had this been *her* great-grandmother, Gram's mother? Her insides trembled. She needed confirmation, and the man who'd learned everything there was to know about this town and its citizens from his folks was seated in the next room.

But Duke Plummer was gone, his newspaper and scissors abandoned as if he'd heard her coming and run. Frustration piled atop the bewilderment and shock gripping Andy. She slumped out of the gloomy building and into the bright day.

The sun was hot, beating relentlessly down, warming her skin but not relieving the chill inside her. Gram had told her the last four generations of her family hailed from eastern Washington. *Was it a lie, Gram?* Andy didn't want to believe that, didn't want to face what it would mean—that Gram might have lied to her about so much more.

But at the moment, everything pointed in that direction.

She shielded her eyes from the sun's glare with her hand and looked up and down Main Street. If Gram's family had once lived here, there had to be someone who knew, some record of it.

The spiral on Alder Gulch Community Church glinted white and silver against the deep blue sky like a fishing lure flashing in a mountain lake. Andy clicked her fingers. Churches had records of births and deaths.

JACK STRODE UP THE RAMP that led to the church's entrance. The double doors were ajar and voices filtered out from inside. Duke Plummer's booming tones were easily recognized, but the other voice was softer and he wasn't sure who was arguing with the museum curator. Jack yanked open the door and stepped into the dark interior.

Sudden silence fell heavily against his ears. Precious seconds elapsed while his eyes adjusted to the change of light. Then he saw it wasn't Andy that Plummer had been arguing with as he'd suspected, but Gene Mott. Where had she gone? He'd seen her heading this way, but he'd been too far behind to call out, so he'd settled for following her.

"Don't let me stop your discussion." Jack moved toward the two men.

Gene closed his eyes and rubbed his temples as if trying to massage away a headache. "It can wait."

Plummer meshed his long fingers together over the cover of the book he was holding. Jack couldn't read the title, but he'd swear it was neither a Bible nor a hymnal. One of Mott's novels? Something from the museum? A photo album? Had they been arguing about something in the book? Or something else?

"If you're looking for Reverend Bissel," Plummer said, "he's not here."

"Actually, I was looking for Ms. Hart. I thought I saw her entering the church a few minutes ago."

Plummer stiffened at this news and exchanged a glance with Gene that Jack could not read and didn't like.

"She's out back," Gene said, gesturing toward the back door. "In the cemetery."

Glad to be away from the two men, Jack stepped out into bright daylight again. An ancient-looking cemetery surrounded by a rusting, wrought-iron fence occupied a patch of land twenty feet back from the church. He spotted Andy immediately.

For five whole seconds, as though his boots were mired in mud, he stood there, watching her move from headstone to headstone.

There was something about her as pure and unaffected as the countryside behind her, and yet she stood out like a wildflower amongst the tumbleweeds. He could see something was troubling her, and he forced himself down the stairs and through the wrought-iron gate that made a mournful squeak as it swung inward.

Andy let out a startled yelp and spun around. Her long dark hair fell softly about her face, emphasizing the startling blue of her eyes. Jack's heart raced like a yearling colt in an open field. "More research?"

"Research?"

Jack frowned. "For your book."

"Sure. The book." But she said it with no conviction.

What had her so upset? Something here? Jack's gaze raked the headstones, but he could pick out nothing to account for

Andy's agitation. "I suppose old cemeteries are good sources for historical names?"

Andy's fingers grazed the crown of a headstone honoring Josiah R. Leach, beloved husband of Enid, devoted father of Abigail Sue and Eloise Ann. Gram's name had been Eloise Ann. Andy had been named after her.

She'd wanted confirmation. Now she had it. She felt as if she'd been blindsided, as weak as a kitten in a windstorm. She gestured toward the church. "Did you know the original church burned to the ground forty years ago?"

"No." Jack shrugged. "But I'm not surprised. Fires are a real hazard in towns like this where water's scarce."

"All their records went up in smoke," she continued in a singsong voice. "But I found what I wanted, anyway."

Jack glanced at the headstone she continued stroking like a pet rabbit, and read the names for enlightenment, but found none.

Andy's eyes met his. They were accusing. "Why do people lie?"

Jack drew a taut breath, his fingers curling into fists. If she expected him to admit he was a liar, she'd be disappointed. Jack Black, down-and-out cowpoke, was far from the first persona he'd taken on in order to get a story. Of course, most times his life hadn't relied on his dishonesty. "Sometimes lying serves a purpose."

She shook her head, her hair shifting across her shoulders. "No matter who gets hurt? Well, I can't abide lying...or liars."

He said nothing.

Andy stared at his inviting mouth, recalling how wonderful his kiss had made her feel, recalling how disappointed she'd been that he hadn't kissed her until she'd begged him to stop, recalling how certain she was that he had lied to her. Just how bad was his lie? "Do you have a wife, Jack? A family?"

The switch of subject was so abrupt, he almost told her he

lived with his mother and his sister's family. "My mother is still alive, and my sister is married, but I've never come close."

"Really?" An incredibly handsome man like him? "Why is that?"

With all his heart and to his profound consternation, he wished he could tell her the whole awful truth, wished he could put an end to his obsession once and for all, wished he could get to know this woman whose kiss had haunted his dreams last night. "How about you? You're not wearing a ring, but then, women don't always in this day and age. A family, a husband, kids?"

"No one." Andy considered mentioning Gram, but the confusion she felt over discovering Gram's lies had filled her with distrust. "No parents, no kids, no husband."

She judged from the uneasy flicker in his eyes that he, too, had been thinking about their kiss and wondering if he'd overstepped his bounds. Feeling a nudge of guilt for betraying Tim, she added, "But I have promised to marry a wonderful guy in Seattle."

A shimmer of pain grazed Jack's chest. Of course she was engaged. A special lady like her. He envied her the happiness ahead. If he ever brought Nightmare Man to justice, he'd seek his own happiness. "Good for you. Don't let anything stand in your way."

Not even me. Especially me. Jack tipped his hat and started to spin away from her when he noticed her arm was bare, her scar exposed for the whole town to see. A shiver crawled the length of his spine, and unintentionally he grasped her left hand and tipped it up to get a better look at her scar.

Andy gazed up at him, fear in her bright blue eyes. Fear of him. Jack felt like a heel. She was not Leandra Woodworth and nothing awful was going to happen to her. "I—"

"What is it with the men in this town?" Andy yanked her hand from his. "Haven't any of you seen a scar before? No.

Don't answer that. I've had all the lies I can handle for one day.'' She stormed out of the graveyard and left him staring after her, breathing in her gentle flowery scent.

ANDY DROVE INTO BUTTE for dinner, the long hours alone on the road giving her time to ponder the reasons for Gram's lies about Montana. It was near midnight when she returned and pulled in to the parking spot of the Motherlode Motel. She was dead tired. All of the rustic cabins were dark, their occupants likely asleep. Alder Gulch closed early.

The night always held an indefinable spookiness for her, and Andy was glad to arrive quickly and safely inside her cabin. Even its ghastly pink walls were a welcome sight.

Within minutes she'd changed into the old T-shirt she slept in, removed her contacts, washed her face and brushed her teeth. She rolled the quilt to the foot of the bed, then pulled back the covers and slipped beneath them. She'd be asleep as soon as her head hit the pillow.

Andy reached toward the bedside lamp and froze.

Something had scuttled from beneath the quilt. Something yellowish brown with two black stripes on its back.

A scorpion.

A scream climbed Andy's throat. The scorpion beelined for her. Terror held her paralyzed. Her gaze riveted on the scorpion's menacing tail, curled, pulsing, primed to deliver its deadly sting.

Chapter Five

The scream tore through Jack's troubled sleep. He bolted upright in bed, his heart pumping like the legs of a runaway bull. Another scream rent the quiet night. His head jerked toward the sound. Next door. Andy! He flung off the covers, grabbed his jeans and hopped into them as he hurried barefoot across the cold cabin floor and out onto the colder ground.

Another scream ripped through the quiet and he sprinted to the porch of the cabin next to his and grasped the doorknob. It was locked. "Andrea! Let me in!"

The door crashed open and she threw herself at him, grasping his neck and scooting her legs up his as if she were shinning up a tree, as if she were trying to get her feet off the floor.

"What the—"

"Shut the door!" she cried. "Quick!"

Catching her to him with one arm, Jack awkwardly seized the knob and slammed the door. The crash rang in the noiseless night. A couple of lights in the cabins beyond Jack's blinked on, but no one ventured out to inquire as to the cause of the disturbance. "Are you okay?"

"Yeah," Andy croaked.

Unconvinced and fearful, Jack hurriedly carried her to his cabin, kicked the door shut behind them and leaned against it, breathing hard. Moonlight cast the room in a golden mist, and for ten long seconds Jack held Andy's head pressed to his naked shoulder, burying his nose in the sweet fragrance of her velvety hair, one hand pressed against the thin cotton fabric at her back, one cupped beneath her firm bottom, which seemed covered only by something sheer and silken. His heart thumped as rapidly as hers. From sudden fright. From the unknown cause of it. From awareness.

That realization got him moving across the room. He set Andy on his disheveled bed and reached for the bedside lamp.

Andy's breath shuddered from her and she pulled her knees to her chest.

Dim light spilled into the room. Jack stood over her. "What happened?"

Andy's chin was on her knees, and her long dark hair fell forward, hiding her face from his as she spoke. "There was a scorpion in my blankets. If I hadn't seen it before I turned off the light—"

She broke off, another shudder rumbling through her.

"Holy—" Jack sank to the bed facing her and gently embraced her.

Andy straightened her legs and nestled her cheek against the springy, silken black hair sparsely adorning Jack's naked chest. He smelled clean and warm and she wanted to climb inside him and let his heat melt the sheet of ice encasing her heart. A scorpion. What a perfectly awful finish to a perfectly awful day.

Jack's hands moved soothingly over her back. "I take it you didn't manage to kill the scorpion?"

"No. I flipped it off the bed onto the floor, but then I couldn't find it. I didn't want to kill it. I just didn't want it to kill me." As she spoke, Andy slowly lifted her head and looked at him.

Jack's mouth dropped open and goose bumps lifted on his naked flesh. *Her eyes.* One was all blue, the other was one-quarter blue and three-quarters brown, as beautiful as a gem stone of lapis lazuli. Just like—

Dear God, Andrea Hart *was* Leandra Woodworth!

Andy grabbed a handful of her long hair just above he forehead and tugged it up and away from her face, an uncon scious yet sensual gesture. She frowned at him. "I thought was the one who'd been frightened—but you're as pale as i you'd seen a ghost."

"I guess you could say I have," he sputtered. "Am. Look ing at one now."

"I beg your pardon." She shifted out of his grasp and bacl against the brass headboard.

The complete incomprehension in her eyes affirmed Jack' suspicions that she didn't know her true identity. And i roused an awful fear in him as he recalled how she'd roame around town that day with her wrist exposed, parading he distinctive scar for one and all to see. Including Nightmar Man.

He clenched his jaw. How had that scorpion gotten into he cabin, into her bed?

"Hello in there." Andy shattered his grim musings. "I'n waiting for an explanation here. Why did you call me ghost?"

How did he tell her? Where did he start? Hell, would sh even believe him? He thought of the trip he'd made into Butt earlier that night, about the background check Wally and h had conducted, and decided she might. Eventually. "You eyes are very unusual."

Her impatience was evident in the tilt of her head. "Gran said my father's were the same."

Jack nodded. Arlo Woodworth had passed his unique ey coloring onto his daughter. "I thought you said you didn' have any family."

"I don't." Andy blinked, her emotions logjammed on th

subject of her grandmother. "Gram passed away two months ago."

Gram. Tonight, Wally and he had checked out the names on the gravestone Andy had been so interested in this afternoon, hours of labor paying off when they'd discovered Arlo Woodworth's mother's maiden name had been Leach. Her given name Eloise Ann. The woman who'd disappeared with Lee Lee.

But even with that link, until he'd looked into her eyes a moment ago, Jack hadn't dared hope that Andrea Hart was the missing Leandra. The shock running through his system seemed to be dissipating and he realized finding Lee Lee might only have aggravated his problems, since she apparently still did not remember that awful, crucial night. But something had brought her here. "After your grandmother's death—is that when you learned of your connection with Alder Gulch?"

"My connection? No. What are you talking about?"

She looked so vulnerable, Jack wanted to pull her close again, but he figured any move in that direction right now would erase whatever trust he'd earned with her. He rubbed his long fingers down the legs of his jeans. "What brought you to Alder Gulch?"

"I told you—research for my new book." Andy glimpsed the ribbon of ebony hair that feathered down Jack's flat stomach and disappeared into the waistband of his jeans. Her mouth watered. She swallowed hard, then forced her gaze to his long, lean fingers, and, even in her agitated confusion, she was aware of how little he wore, how little she wore, how wonderfully comforting nestling against his bare chest felt....

"So, you just picked this town out of a hat?" Jack's sage green eyes were dark with a concern she didn't understand.

"No. In the past seven weeks I've visited seven ghost towns. This one just hit my hot button—" She broke off, her mind finally engaging, churning and connecting, digesting and processing. "Why did you suggest I might have heard of Alder Gulch at the time of Gram's death?"

"Well…" Jack braced his arms on his thighs and leaned closer to her, wishing she didn't smell so sweet, so damned divertingly like a dessert he couldn't indulge in. No distractions. He had to remember that she held the solution to his obsession locked in her mind, had to remember he might not be able to set it free, had to remember if he did succeed, it could unleash the devil's wrath on them both.

At least *he'd* come into this with his eyes wide open. Andy was naive to the dangers, and Jack hated the unpleasant necessity of stripping her of her innocence. "I have reason to believe your real name is Leandra Woodworth and that you were born and raised in this town until the age of five, when your parents were brutally murdered."

She stared openmouthed at him. "Really, Jack. And you accused me of having a big imagination. My parents died in a car crash."

"How do you know that?"

"Gram told me." Even as she said it, Andy felt the old panic come alive and burgeon through her chest and pound against her temples.

"You know your grandmother lied to you about your past." Jack's voice rose an octave. "You discovered it today—at that tombstone."

"You're nuts." Andy laughed, but she felt no mirth. Yesterday she'd been certain who she was, but now… Gram *had* lied to her. No doubt there. But murder? Impossible.

She shook her head at Jack. "I told you earlier that I'd had all the lies I could stand, so where do you get off asking me to believe anything you say when you couldn't tell the truth if you had to, Jack Sta-Black?"

Jack's sigh was loud as he raked his hands through his hair. "My real name is Jack Starett, Jr.—rancher and restaurateur."

Andy crossed her arms over her chest. "And you want to know what *I'm* doing in Alder Gulch?"

Jack sighed, obviously struggling with himself about something. At length, he said, "I've spent the past fifteen years looking for the man who murdered my father. The same man who murdered your parents. I have every reason to believe he resides in this very town. A man you once dubbed 'Nightmare Man.'"

Something cold and slimy crawled out of a murky corner deep in Andy's mind, something as awful and terrifying as a child's worst dream. Panic pounded at her temples and she gulped for air, gasped for it. "No! No! You're lying. I'm not Leandra Woodworth."

She lurched away from Jack, scrambled off the opposite side of the bed and over to one of the windows, flinging it open for air. Hugging herself, she threw back her head and drew a steadying breath.

Bright light poked her eyes, and she noticed the moon was as round and full as a supper plate in the sky. Without warning, a voice sounded inside her head, Gram's voice. "That's a good old Montana fool's moon, Lee Lee."

"Oh, God!" Andy sobbed. "Oh, Gram! How deep did the lies go?"

Jack stepped up behind her and wrapped his arms around her, glad that she didn't resist, sensing she was close to collapse. "You remembered something?"

"Yes."

"Nightmare Man's identity?" Jack held his breath.

"No. Maybe never. My doctor said I was blocking out what happened to my parents because I couldn't bear the trauma."

"Hysterical amnesia." Jack's sigh rang with defeat.

She spun around in his arms and faced him.

Jack loosened his stance, but kept his large hands warmly on her shoulders. He seemed unusually tense, and Andy was suddenly cold, chilled to the bone, but this cold was not induced by weather, this cold arose from inside her. "You're worried if I don't quit hiding behind my fear and expose him, Nightmare Man will come after me."

Jack's Adam's apple bobbed as if whatever he had to say was choking him.

What didn't he want to tell her? But as she wondered, the scorpion scurrying across the bed at her flashed into Andy's mind, and she knew. "You think he already has, don't you?"

Chapter Six

"The scorpion, Jack." The certainty of it wobbled her knees and grabbed her stomach in a knot of fear. "You think *he* planted it in my bed, don't you?"

With tenderness that belied his size, Jack smoothed his hands across her shoulders, down her arms and cupped her elbows, steadying her. His face betrayed his concern. "Let's not jump to conclusions."

Andy shook her head. "No more lies. Not between us. Not even to save my sanity. Agreed?"

Jack's scowl fell into place and Andy had the bizarre urge to reach up and massage it away. Several seconds passed, ticked off by the anxious thudding of her heart against her rib cage, the whine of the wind stealing through the open window at her back and the thoughtful flutter of Jack's dense ebony lashes as he seemed to consider myriad consequences of complete honesty with her.

Finally he nodded. "My instinct is pretty much the same as your grandmother's—get you as far away from this town as fast as possible. But I'm not certain that would protect you. Not now. Of course, the scorpion might just have wandered inside of its own accord. I'll have a better idea after I get a look at it. However, I'm not keen on trying to find it in a cabin with only lamplight as a guide. First thing tomorrow."

First thing tomorrow. Andy shuddered, and Jack eased her

against him. She circled her arms around him, her hands splaying against his naked back, her cool cheek resting against his warm, strong chest. She sought comfort, reassurance, but he smelled so deliciously clean, like the freshest spring day, every cell in her body seemed alert, tingling with awareness.

The chill inside her lessened and although she sensed the danger of her feelings, her longings, her vulnerable state of undress, she couldn't bring herself to pull away. Only in fiction had she experienced such a heady, sensuous touch. Only in her fantasies had she dreamed a woman's total arousal. Why hadn't she experienced this with Tim?

Guilt wedged itself between Andy and her feelings. Self-consciously she shoved away from Jack. "It's getting chilly in here."

A blush warmed her cheeks at the lie and, not wanting him to notice it, Andy quickly reached for the window. She gazed one last time at the moon, and a lump of desperation tightened her throat. Would she ever remember the horror of her parents' deaths? She prayed not.

She latched the window and wheeled around. Jack was standing beside the bed, smoothing the rumpled covers. Andy's self-consciousness returned in a rush. Except for the pale blue walls and the lack of a desk, this cabin was an exact replica of hers. No couch, no comfortable chairs to sack out on, only one narrow, antique brass bed that didn't look large enough for Jack.

"Don't even offer to sleep in the bathtub," Jack said, shaking his head. "I've never understood the logic in that. Just end up with a crick in your neck and tailbone. I'll take the floor."

"No!" The word jumped out of her. "I can't let you do that. What if this motel is infested with scorpions? You could get stung. No. We can share the bed. I'll sleep on top of the covers and you can sleep under them."

A lopsided grin tugged at Jack's sensuous mouth and his

sexy gaze swept the length of her. "You'd catch your death in that outfit."

Andy tugged ineffectually on the hem of her T-shirt and was immediately sorry as she realized the gesture accentuated her naked breasts beneath.

"Besides," Jack added, the sudden huskiness in his voice sending sweet shivers through her, "you're putting a lot of trust in a man you hardly know."

It was true. She hardly knew him. He'd lied to her from the first moment they'd met, and, despite that, she did trust him. Had no choice but to trust him. "I'll accept your word as a gentleman."

A lustful glint danced in his eyes. "Black Jack Black is no gentleman, ma'am."

Andy arched an eyebrow at him and smiled. "Something tells me Jack Starett, Jr., is."

Confirming her belief, Jack insisted she get under the covers, then he climbed on top of them and pulled the quilt over himself. The bedsprings squeaked like rusty wagon wheels as they settled down, Andy propping herself against the headboard with a pillow, Jack stretching on his side facing her.

His bare feet poked out the bottom of the quilt and Andy feared if either of them flipped over during the night the other would end up on the floor. However, there was something strangely comfortable about the moment, almost like times Gram and she had talked in bed late at night, and despite her battered, lonely heart, despite the lingering terror of old memories, there was something indefinable about Jack—maybe the mere size of him—that gave her a sense of security.

Yet there was so much she didn't know about him. "How did…the same man come to murder your father?"

Sadness touched his face and she could see he'd loved his father devotedly.

"Dad was a top-notch investigative reporter working out

of the offices of the *Butte Sun*. He covered the story on the murder of your parents, writing a couple of heart-wrenching, human-interest pieces about the only witness to the brutal murder of her parents—the little girl who couldn't remember anything of the tragedy, except the name Nightmare Man.''

Andy closed her eyes, fighting off the nausea provoked by the vile name. She still didn't remember anything about the tragedy. She believed Jack was telling her the truth; her reaction to the name Nightmare Man was proof enough. Any newspaper would certainly have an account on record, but the whole idea that someone had murdered her parents seemed unreal.

The facts as Jack stated them wouldn't slot comfortably into her mind. Instead they kept popping out, scattering through her head like the contents of an overturned drawer, demanding attention. Pain tweaked her temples and she scrubbed her face with her hands. The trouble was, she couldn't visualize any of it. She didn't even have a photograph of her parents, didn't even recall what they had looked like.

Jack shifted on the bed, setting off the springs as he drew the quilt higher on his bare shoulder. Were these memories also chilling him? He said, "Then you disappeared. Stolen out of town in the dead of night by your grandmother."

Andy twisted her hands together in her lap, and an ancient pain centered in her heart. How could something that had happened so long ago still hurt so much? "I can vaguely recall waking up in a strange bed—a motel room somewhere—with Gram by my side."

"Wallingford Lester, the editor of the *Sun*, was a cub reporter working under my dad at the time. He said Dad told him your grandmother was terrified for you. The police offered protection, but when the officer on duty let some thrill-seeking little ghoul past him, she knew the police would never keep you safe."

Andy's logjammed emotions burst, wrenching a groan from her. She fought against the pain constricting her throat and the tears burning her eyes. "Why did…he kill your dad?"

"A man who wouldn't identify himself called Dad at the *Sun* demanding to know your whereabouts. Dad guessed the caller was Nightmare Man and he was certain he recognized the voice. Apparently, while Wally was out of the office, Dad checked it out. Somehow he must have tipped his hand, because he didn't make it home that night. He was found three days later, his car parked on the side of the road. He'd been killed the same way as your mother." Jack's voice broke.

Icy dread plunged through Andy. Jack hadn't even seen his father murdered and just talking about it shook him to his core. She dug her nails into her palms. What would happen to her if she recalled the ugly memories buried deep in her subconscious? The mere idea set her temples throbbing and she knew she couldn't put herself through that. "I'm so sorry about your dad, Jack."

"You're lucky your grandmother acted as quickly as she did."

"Yeah." Andy smiled wanly. *How can I stay mad at you, Gram? You saved my life.*

There was hope in Jack's expression. "If you could only recall his face."

The suggestion rekindled her panic and it was twenty seconds before Andy controlled the urge to leap out of bed and run. He might like her to remember, but he couldn't force her to. No one could. "I don't even remember what my parents looked like."

"Well, I can help you there. There are some old photographs at the news office. I'll have Wally send them to you."

Andy flinched. A part of her rejoiced at the idea, but a bigger part feared the photographs would trigger the very memories she'd rather not recall. She was quiet for a moment, aware of the gentle rise and fall of Jack's chest, of his utter nearness, of how comfortable the silence was. "Why didn't Gram tell me the truth when I grew up?"

Jack shrugged. "Maybe your doctor warned her not to."

Andy thought of Dr. Santini and decided Jack was probably right in that assumption. The elderly psychiatrist had been almost as overly protective of her as Gram.

Jack snuggled down into his pillow. Tiredness etched lines in the corners of his eyes and around his mouth, that warm, sweet-tasting, nerve-tingling mouth. She wanted him to kiss her again, to see if she'd imagined the sensations, and she guessed he was thinking along the same lines. But he said, "Tomorrow we'll figure out some way of getting you back to Seattle in one piece."

"Yes." Disappointed, Andy scooted down and bumped against Jack in the narrow bed. She murmured a hasty apology. Tomorrow she'd call Tim.

"Night." Jack blew a sigh, turned away from her and doused the light.

"Night." Andy rolled to her side, her back to Jack, her nose buried in the pillow that smelled wonderfully of his aftershave, her body silently begging him to roll over and make love to her. But he didn't, and she supposed she ought to be grateful that Jack Starett, Jr., was truly a gentleman. *You would have liked him, Gram.*

Sleep teased her, but fearing she would dream of the scorpion, Andy concentrated on the scene she was working on in her story and soon she was romping with her heroine through the gold-mining days of yesteryear.

MOONLIGHT FELL across Andy's face. She opened her sleep-clogged eyes, blinking against the sudden brightness, wondering where she was. She sat up and realized she was in bed. The light spilling through the room told her it was a bedroom from her childhood. Toys lay scattered on the floor. Inexplicably, she shivered and hugged her arms around her middle, somehow expecting disaster.

It came with a shriek like a hoot owl's screech rending the peaceful night and filling Andy with such terror it stole her voice. A smothering silence followed. Then a loud crash jolted through the quiet and Andy jumped from the bed.

Odd that she'd told Jack she couldn't recall what either of her parents looked like. She could see them quite clearly now, see exactly what had happened to them.

From behind her, a man said, "Lee Lee."

Andy's heart jolted. Nightmare Man. Without looking at his face, she ran from his grasp. But he kept chasing her, calling, "Lee Lee."

Without knowing how she'd gotten there, she huddled in some dark, familiar corner, crying, softly whimpering, "Mommy."

Her wrist stung with pain. But there was a deeper pain inside her, and a fear like none she'd felt before. She sniffled and caught an alien scent.

What was that odd, smoky smell, that funny whooshing crackling like...fire? Through teary eyes she realized the door of her hiding place was ajar. She could see the dining room table. Smoke, like thunderclouds inside the house, billowed toward the ceiling and she guessed it was the source of the smarting in her nostrils. Why was there so much smoke? Puzzled, she watched as flames leapt across the lace runner and climbed Grammy's crocheted centerpiece.

Suddenly Andy understood what she was looking at. Her eyes flew wide open. With a squeal of terror she shoved the large sack of dog food aside. She had to get out, out of the pantry, out of the house. But something or someone was holding her down. Nightmare Man! She lashed out, trying to hit his face. To hurt him as he'd hurt her.

Jack's voice cut through the terror. Andy opened her eyes. She was sobbing—dry, bone-jarring sobs. She quit fighting, let Jack pull her close, and eventually choked out, ''I remember...the house was on fire. I had to get out...to the safe place.''

''You're safe now,'' Jack said, reaching for and switching on the bedside lamp, recalling how light in the dark of night could take the edge off a nightmare, could offer a sobering sense of time and place. Some perspective.

But she was trembling like a fever victim, and he knew it would take more than a dose of tangibility to help Andy right now.

Shaking uncontrollably, she shoved herself away from him. She stared at the scar on her wrist. Oddly, it stung as if the wound were freshly inflicted. She could almost see the blood dripping from the gashes.

''I am Lee Lee Woodworth,'' she said, admitting to herself that she hadn't fully believed it until now. She shuddered and pressed her palms to her temples, trying to squeeze out the shattering images from her dream. Instead of leaving, the visions heightened, defined themselves, became more vivid with every revealed detail. She moaned. ''No, no, no.''

''What can I do?'' Jack's voice rang with worry. ''Andy, let me help you.''

But there was nothing he could do. Jack couldn't make the heinous visions disappear—because they weren't visions at all, they were memories, they were what she'd seen when she was five, what Nightmare Man had done to her parents.

With acceptance came a raging fury—and terror more intimidating than any nightmare she'd ever had, that grabbed her chest and sucked away the very foundations of her existence, of every truth she had ever known.

Nothing could keep her safe. Nothing and no one. Panic stole her breath. She batted at Jack's outstretched arms, scrambled off the bed and ran into the bathroom.

Jack chased after her, but she slammed the door. Swearing at the pain he knew she was suffering, he slumped against the wall, feeling powerless, useless. The sound of running water in the sink was followed by the toilet being flushed. Jack thought he heard Andy retching.

Fifteen minutes later she came out, her face a mask of white. "I have to get out of here. I have to get away."

"All right." Jack nodded, then gestured to her T-shirt. "But where do you think you're going like that?"

"You can lend me something."

"Anything, anytime. But my shirts won't offer you any more coverage than the one you're wearing, and I haven't anything else that will fit you. Do you want me to get you something from your cabin?"

The thought of Jack running into the scorpion was more than she could deal with. The scorpion and how and why it had been in her bed robbed the fight from Andy. She shook her head. Hot tears filled her eyes and streamed down her cheeks and into her mouth, tasting salty, coppery. She turned her pleading gaze to Jack, willing him to understand. But one look into those sage green eyes and she realized he did understand, had already traveled the ground she was traveling now.

He opened his arms. Andy collapsed against him, sobbing. Jack lifted her like a child and carried her back to the bed. He murmured sweetly, softly, but Andy didn't hear the words, just the tone of his voice, which her fragile spirit latched on to, a reassuring monotone that offered hope and encouragement, comfort and strength. The awful sense of impending peril dwindled.

For the next two hours, in fits and starts, she told Jack what she had remembered—which was everything except Nightmare Man's identity.

When she'd gotten it all out, she felt drained, yet oddly relieved. And exhausted. She closed her eyes, curling against Jack's big, protective body.

She had no idea how long she'd slept, but now sunlight

caressed the windows as lightly as Jack was tracing the contours of her back with strong yet gentle strokes that warmed everywhere he touched. Andy realized she wanted to pull his strength, his gentleness, his warmth inside her until it revived the part of her soul the memories of Nightmare Man had killed.

She nuzzled Jack's hands just as Minna's white-pawed cat—so like her beloved Boots—had nuzzled her leg the day she'd checked in. Except she doubted the cat had ever been half as needy as she felt at this moment.

Every stroke, every grazing touch of Jack's was like balm soothed into her parched soul. She sighed softly, appreciatively, and then her gaze met his. The empathy she saw there reaffirmed her belief that he'd been here. He knew. He'd felt everything she was feeling now. She reached out to him with her heart, with her mind, knowing full well she could trust him as she'd never trusted another, knowing full well her yearning was reflected in her eyes.

Jack groaned as if he were in pain and cupped her face with his big hands. "Are you sure?"

Andy answered by lifting her lips to his, surprising herself with her eagerness, her hunger, abandoning herself to the fiery sensations sweeping through her, and soon the chunk of ice around her heart began melting like heated butter.

His work-roughened hands stroked the tender flesh of her thighs, moved under her T-shirt, over her silk panties, across her midriff to her breasts, his grainy fingertips rousing her nipples to aching peaks, every stroke a wicked, shimmery friction of coarse skin against tender skin making her feel more alive than she'd ever felt.

Her heart beat with a speed born of pleasure and need, washing her most secret places with longing—longing for a fulfillment she'd never experienced, didn't totally believe was possible. She arched into his hand. "Oh, Jack."

He kissed her neck, pressing his body closer, offering Andy

the hard proof of his desire for her, hearing her rapid breathing through the pulse thundering in his ears, feeling her thrumming heart against his palm. He wanted her as he'd never wanted any woman.

The thought stunned Jack, sobered him. It wasn't love she wanted, and she sure as hell didn't need any more complications in her life right now. Hell, she didn't even want him. Not really. Any man would do. She wasn't thinking, she was reacting.

"No. We can't do this." Jack disentangled himself from her arms. His voice was a raspy violin chord of unspent ardor. "You're engaged."

Blowing out a frustrated sigh, he collapsed on the pillow, his arms behind his head as he stared at the ceiling.

Confused and breathless, Andy plopped on the pillow beside him, staring at the same ceiling. Her face felt flushed with unspent passion. For several minutes the only sound in the cabin was their uneven breathing.

Sunlight had crept higher on the windowpane, casting golden beams on the wall and floor. Jack was right. She hadn't been thinking clearly. Andy swallowed hard, her cheeks burning at how close she'd come to losing complete control. The one saving grace, she realized, was that her fear had lessened to a level she could manage.

Jack said, "Did you get a good look at the scorpion? Could you describe it to me?"

Andy blinked at the unexpected question, then glanced over and up at him. "I don't know—it looked like that one at the Golden Broom bar."

Imagining the scorpion again raised goose bumps on her arms and legs. She forced her focus elsewhere, studying Jack's face, which was in dire need of a shave. She'd bet he could grow a fair beard in a week. It gave him a fearsome look, but she'd glimpsed his heart and knew there was a tender side to Jack Starett, Jr., that one wouldn't suspect at first glance.

He lurched off the bed, its springs protesting until he'd reached the dresser. Within minutes he'd donned his boots and was snapping the pearl buttons of yet another Western-style black shirt. "Before we make any decisions about your future, I need a look at that scorpion."

"I want to help."

"All right. I'll bring you some clothes."

While Jack was gone, Andy considered what he'd said about her future. Of course, if Nightmare Man had already discovered she was Leandra Woodworth—she might not have a future. The realization astounded her. But she wouldn't be the first woman who'd faced such a dilemma.

As she recalled, a popular actress on a daytime soap opera had been forced to give up her career, her right to a normal existence, because of an obsessed fan's persistent threats to kill her. Hearing the story, Andy's heart had gone out to the woman, who, still in hiding, no longer even dared receive mail.

In the bathroom Andy washed her face with cold water. She gazed at her reflection in the mirror, trying to imagine hiding out the rest of her life, never having a telephone, never getting mail.

A sickening clamminess swept her.

She gulped down cold water from the tap. That kind of existence meant giving up her goals, her dreams, giving up the books she still wanted to write, giving up all thoughts of marrying, raising a family. Living. Impotent rage shook her to her toes. If that was all her life would ever be, she might as well let Nightmare Man kill her.

Jack rapped on the bathroom door. "Your clothes."

"Thanks." She was glad to see he'd brought her contacts as well as fresh underwear, jeans, a long-sleeved blouse and high-topped sneakers. Certain he'd already done so, she nonetheless checked each item before donning it. She put in her contacts, used his comb on her hair, then joined him in the main room.

Jack was sitting on the bed, waiting.

She said, "I've made a decision. Even if Nightmare Man did put the scorpion in my bed—" she hesitated, bracing for his inevitable protest "—I'm not leaving here."

"What?" Jack's long, vacant scowl surfaced. "Why?"

"The last images of my mother and father will stay with me no matter where I go, hovering in the forefront of my mind, spurring me to remember and bring their murderer to justice. I expect you've suffered something similar since your father's murder." The chill inside her had returned, but now it held a steel shaft of resolve. She'd thought hard about this, considered every option, every consequence. There was only one way to lay the images to rest, to ever have the life she wanted. "I've got to remember who he is."

This was exactly what Jack had prayed for day after day through all the years of his obsession—his father's murderer brought to justice. Andy's way insured that justice. Nightmare Man would not escape the proof of the only witness. Then why did Jack feel as if his guts were being torn from him? He raked his hands through his hair. The answer was obvious: fear. One look at her innocent, precious face and he knew he couldn't risk her life. Couldn't let her risk it. "I won't allow you to put yourself in mortal jeopardy."

"You don't have a choice in the matter. Either you let me help you or I'll strike out on my own investigation."

"Andy, no." At his plea, her chin snapped up, and she arched a determined brow at him. He had to talk some sense into her. "Why don't you return to Seattle, marry that fiancé of yours, then if you remember who Nightmare Man is—"

"Let's not argue." He wasn't talking her out of this. No one was. She squared her shoulders and headed for the door. "Come on, Jack. We have a scorpion to catch."

All the lights were on inside her cabin. She thanked Jack for that and followed him inside, stepping gingerly, her gaze darting toward walls and ceiling where she half expected to see the scorpion hanging or perched overhead somewhere, waiting in ambush.

"Scorpions are shy." Jack strode to the kindling piled beside the stove. "They like dark hiding places."

Andy shivered.

"Like corners," Jack said, tumbling the stacked wood with the toe of his boot, quickly hunkering down and scanning the floor for some sign of movement.

"Or behind desks." Warily, Andy heaved the desk away from the wall and peered behind it. No scorpion.

"Or under the covers." Jack yanked blankets and sheets from the bed and dumped them to the floor, then lifted the mattress, rousing a piteous squeaking from the old bed frame.

Andy noticed the dictionary on her desk had a gap between the pages—as if it held some foreign object. With shaking fingers she grasped the book by its cover and, holding it at arm's length, shook it.

A pencil tumbled to the floor at the same moment someone rapped on the door. Andy jolted, dropping the book in a heap. She blushed, feeling foolish. She'd known she was tense, but this was ridiculous. Laughing at herself, she bent over to retrieve the book and called, "Come in."

Minna Kroft swung the door inward, smacking the wall behind it with a bang. She glanced from Jack to Andy, her amber eyes narrowing in puzzlement beneath her fluffy gray hair, making her look every bit as curious as any of her cats. "Guest in number eleven claims they was a ruckus down here the middle of the night."

"I wouldn't call it a ruckus," Andy said.

"She just had a bad dream," Jack added, wondering if Minna Kroft had allowed someone to put the scorpion in

Andy's bed, hoping Andy would take the hint and let Minna give herself away if she had.

"I'm afraid I overreacted to it." Andy brushed off the dictionary and returned it to the desk.

"So, whatcha doin' now?" Minna stepped into the cabin, obviously disapproving of the mess they'd made.

"Well," Jack said, scrambling for an innocent explanation, "we—"

"What the—?" Minna cut him off. She was glancing at the floor near her foot, her slanted eyes rounded. Jack's gaze dropped to the floor. Minna drew a startled indrawn breath that sounded like a squawk. "Ye gods!"

Before Jack or Andy could stop her, Minna stomped her heavy gardening boot down on the creature as it scuttled toward her. The clomp echoed through the room, followed by a distasteful crunch as she ground her boot into the pink-and-gray floor, completely annihilating the scorpion, and any way of proving it had ever existed.

Minna was clutching her chest. "Danged nasty critters."

Fury leapt inside Jack. Minna had reacted with the speed of lightning, or was it the speed of guilt? Had it been the natural reaction to a deadly creature—or had she killed the scorpion for reasons of her own? Jack struggled to keep his voice level. "I wish you hadn't done that, Mrs. Kroft."

"Are ya loco?" Minna looked astonished. "I'll have ya know, young man, my aunt died from the bite of one of them critters."

"The sting," Andy said, still visualizing the curled tail.

Minna glanced at her, eyebrows twitching. "What?"

"Scorpions don't bite," Andy explained. "They sting."

Minna puffed an aggravated breath. "Aunt Hetty's dead jest the same."

"Was her death recent?" Jack took a step closer.

"Lands, no." Minna shook her head, setting her hair to

waving. "Happened when I was a girl. Never forgot it though."

"Did it happen here in Alder Gulch?" Jack gathered the covers from the floor, tossed them onto the bare mattress and moved to Andy's side.

"Nope. Florida." A puzzled expression twisted Minna's feline features. "Ain't that curious. I never heard tell of scorpions in this here county. Winters is too cold. Where do ya suppose it come from?"

Jack shrugged. He, too, had never heard of scorpions in this part of Montana. He'd decided not to mention that to Andy last night, but he could see the questions in her eyes now, could see that she knew he'd never suspected the scorpion had gotten into her bed by itself. Jack hated the fear that realization was likely causing her.

The minute Minna left them alone, Andy rounded on Jack. She didn't ask whether the scorpion was native to this part of Montana or—as he half expected—berate him for not telling her.

"Let's go to the Golden Broom." Instead of fear, there was a new determination in her voice. "I want to see if Red Yager is missing any scorpions."

The earlier promise of a sunny day had given way to thick black clouds and a brisk, cold breeze. Andy hugged herself as they stepped from the path onto Main Street. Few tourists occupied the wooden sidewalks, fewer cars the road.

Wind whined between the aged buildings, whistling eerily as if the town were actually deserted, inhabited only by the ghosts of outlaws and gold miners who had roamed this countryside a century ago. Yesterday she would have treasured this day for the ambience it would add to her new book, but today her mind was directed elsewhere.

Breakfast was being served in the dining room as well as in the bar of the Golden Broom Hotel. There were fewer diners than the night before, but the noise level was just as high and the clatter of dishes and voices conflicted with the player piano, further jarring her already frayed nerves. Even the wonderful smells didn't tempt Andy; her stomach was one big knot.

She followed Jack, weaving between tables and diners, trying unsuccessfully to keep up with his great long strides. "Jack, slow down. We don't want to draw attention to ourselves."

Jack stiffened, then stopped and waited until she was by his side before starting out again, this time at a relaxed pace. Anxiety knotted his gut. He just wanted to get this over with, get her packed up, see the taillights of her Cherokee headed out of town.

The glass tank stood as usual on the end of the bar, occupying the exact same spot it had the first time Andy had asked him about it. He ordered two black coffees from the bartender, then edged closer to the tank, covertly studying it.

The lid was in place, tightly tacked down. A sign seemed unmoved—Deadly Scorpion. Approach At Your Own Risk—nailed to one edge of the tank to attract and titillate tourists, usually children. Sand covered the bottom of the tank, and a fist-sized rock and a hunk of bark occupied opposite corners.

There was no sign of the scorpion. In fact, the tank appeared empty. Andy shoved a cup of coffee toward him, but Jack didn't notice. Chilly fingers of fear were wrapping his heart and no amount of hot coffee could melt the ice.

Nightmare Man knew Andy was Leandra Woodworth. There would be no keeping her safe now.

"Hey, mister, move over." A boy of about eight elbowed Jack aside. "See this tank, Lisa."

"Aw, there's nothin' in there, Tommy," groused the boy's companion, a girl of about the same age.

Tommy thumped the tank with his fist. "There it is. Under the bark. Look! Look at its tail! I told you so."

"Yuck." Lisa shrank away. "It's creepy."

Andy was staring at the tank, the expression in her eyes unreadable, but Jack recognized the determined set of her jaw. For half a second he'd dared to hope. But he should have known better. There would be no getting her to leave now. He cursed under his breath. "Damn."

Chapter Seven

"Something wrong with my coffee?" Red Yager asked.

Jack's worried thoughts about Andy scattered. He jerked toward the source of the interruption, his stomach as jittery as a jar of jumping beans.

"I think Jack burned his tongue." Andy patted Jack's arm. "The coffee is hot but delicious, Red."

Jack couldn't believe how quickly Andy recouped from the upset, couldn't believe her poise in light of the night she'd had. Sometime this morning she'd found a core of solid steel inside herself. But was it made of courage, or vengeance?

Deciding he'd better get a grip on his own composure, Jack reached for his untasted coffee and studied Red, who stood behind the bar, smelling strongly of Old Spice, his mustache twitching. Jack pointed to the tank containing the scorpion. "I was just wondering how you came by this nasty fellow, Red."

Red squinted at the tank, then shifted an uneasy gaze between Jack and Andy. "Why are you asking?"

Jack hunkered down, settled both forearms on the bar and curled his fingers around his cup, breathing in the rich aroma wafting up from it. "You certainly didn't get it around here."

Thunder rumbled overhead, drawing "oohs" from the diners in the room at Jack's back.

Red swallowed over his Adam's apple and poured himself a cup of coffee. "It was a gift."

"Really?" Jack lifted his own cup and sipped, relishing the heat the coffee sent through his middle as he swallowed. "Mind if I ask who from?"

Red looked on the verge of inquiring again why Jack wanted to know, but he just sniffed and reached for a pint of half-and-half. "Duke Plummer," he said in a lowered voice as if divulging a secret.

"The museum curator?" Andy sounded incredulous.

Red gulped his coffee, leaving his mustache wet. "Ole Duke likes preserving more than the past. In his spare time he tinkers with taxidermy, and in the winter he rides his Harley all across the country. Brought four of these guys home with him last year."

"Four scorpions?" Andy shuddered. "Whatever for?"

"Well, he gave one to me, and one to someone else." Red shrugged. "Maybe he's gonna stuff the two he kept."

Jack wanted to pull Andy close, to somehow ease her dismay.

But her attention was all for Red. She rubbed her wrist, her eyes narrowing. "Do you know who else received a scorpion from Plummer?"

Red scrunched his face in thought for a full five seconds. "'Fraid I don't recall ever being told that."

Jack didn't believe him. But there was no way he could call Red on it without raising questions about himself.

Thunder rumbled in the distance and the pitter-pat of raindrops hitting hard-packed earth floated in through the swinging doors. Jack shoved his and Andy's mugs toward Red. "Why don't you refill these? Then we'll find a table and order some breakfast."

IF JACK HAD HAD HIS WAY, he'd be glued to her side still. But, rainfall or no, the players required his services. After promising not to visit the museum on her own, Andy had left him standing outside the Golden Broom, his face as dark as the clouds overhead. *You should have seen him, Gram.* She laughed. *Black Jack—the name certainly fit him today.*

Watch your step. And don't trust anyone. Jack's words of caution stole the cheer from her as she moved cautiously along the path and hurried unharmed to her cabin. She unlocked the door and stared at the mess they'd left. Memories of the night before, all that she'd learned and felt, including almost making love to Jack, assailed her. Andy stepped across the threshold. She would not think about being afraid. Fear robbed intelligence—and if she were to survive, she needed her wits intact.

But Jack was another matter. For the first time in her life she realized that what she knew about man-woman relationships she'd either learned from television and the movies or made up in her head. Gram had never remarried. Andy had had no real-life examples of what comprised a happy, successful union. Still, before meeting Jack, she'd thought she knew what love was. But did she?

She carried her purse to the desk and set it down. Did she love Tim enough to lay her life on the line for him? Did Tim love her that way? She doubted it. Yet, somehow, she felt Jack, whom she'd known less than forty-eight hours, would. What did that mean? An achy loneliness tugged her heartstrings. "I wish you were here, Gram."

"Andy?"

She stiffened, thinking Gram had answered her, realizing a split second later that the raspy female voice belonged to Minna Kroft. *Don't trust anyone.* Andy pasted a smile on her face and, braced for anything, spun around.

Minna was holding an armful of fresh linens. "Thought ya could use some help settin' things aright."

The phoniness left Andy's smile as she relaxed a modicum. "That's not necessary. I made the mess, I can clean it up."

"Nonsense. Ya look all tuckered out."

The truth was, she'd rather no one else had access to this cabin. Who knew what they might make off with, or leave behind? But Minna shuffled across the room and placed the sheets on the kitchen table. "Work always goes quicker with help."

Andy realized it was unrealistic to think she could keep the motel owner from coming into this cabin whenever she wanted. Besides, Jack couldn't seriously suspect Minna Kroft of being Nightmare Man. Andy closed the cabin door.

"Keep a sharp eye out for hostile creatures," she warned as they gingerly shook out and bundled the soiled bed linen. "Caution is my new motto."

"It's a good one." Minna restacked the wood and swept the floor, while Andy attacked her desk. "There's lotsa beastly critters in this part of Montana."

"Such as?" Andy asked absently, not so much interested in the wildlife of Montana as much as she liked the sound of Minna's voice, the succor of her company.

Minna said, "There's rattlesnakes and wolverines and grizzlies."

Andy came across the packet of glossy prints she'd bought from Coop. Her heart caught. The special photograph. She no longer wondered who the man was; she'd seen his face in her nightmare last night. It was her father—Arlo Woodworth. But the nightmare image of him made her stomach lurch unpleasantly. She wanted to see him as he'd been in the picture Gram had saved, see his face so full of life.

She searched through the packet of prints. Hadn't she put it here yesterday? She frowned, perplexed. It wasn't here now. Perhaps she'd only thought about putting it with the others. Yesterday hadn't exactly been uneventful. She dug through her purse. But the photograph wasn't there, either. She peered behind the desk, then under the bed. Nothing.

"Whatcha lookin' fer?"

"A photograph—of a bearded man, standing before an assay office. Have you seen anything like it?"

"Nope." Minna swept a small pile of dust to the door.

Andy wondered fleetingly if Minna was lying—if her photograph was even now in one of the pockets of her oversized sweater.

"Was it important to yer new book?"

The question was asked with such genuine innocence, Andy felt ashamed of herself for her unkind thoughts about Minna. "It was incredibly important to the book." But irreplaceable to Andy. Disquiet crawled over her as she shuffled through the prints a second time and still did not find her precious photograph.

Think, Andy. Where did you have it last? Fighting against the panic building inside her, she closed her eyes and mentally retraced her actions upon returning from the graveyard yesterday. Her eyes flew open. She'd removed the photograph from her purse and sat at this very desk comparing it with the similar one she'd found at Virgil Cooper's.

When she'd left for dinner, the photograph of her father had been right on the top of the stack, paper-clipped to an exterior shot of the Golden Broom Hotel. She reached a trembling hand into the strewn pile of glossies and quickly extracted the photograph of the hotel. Her chest ached. The paper clip still clung to one edge, hanging on a corner that looked as though it had been torn by someone hastily separating the two photographs. Ice spread through her belly.

Someone had taken her father's picture. Doubtless the same someone who'd put the scorpion in her bed. But taking the picture made no sense. Her knees wobbled. No, it did make sense, a crazy, awful kind of sense. Whoever had killed her parents would have recognized her father at once. Would have wondered where she'd come by the picture. Would probably have figured it out by now.

God help me, Gram. He's one step ahead of me. Somehow I have to pass him, somehow I have to remember.

"Well, now." Minna's raspy voice sliced through Andy's desperation as effectively as the swipe of a knife through Jell-O. "Sweepin's done. Reckon I'll get this stuff to the laundry room."

Minna set aside the broom and gathered the bed linen.

"I'm coming with you. I need to use your telephone." Andy grabbed one of the glossy prints, shrugged into her denim jacket and followed Minna outside.

The white-pawed cat stood on the porch, its fur damp from the misty rain.

"Off with ya, ya ornery puss." Minna kicked her foot in the air above the cat.

The cat didn't budge.

Andy hesitated, clutching the glossy print against her thundering heart. "Hello, Boots. Have you come to make friends?"

The cat eyed her indifferently. Andy squatted and reached a hand to pet its wet head. The cat flinched, leapt off the porch and darted behind the cabin, heading off across the knolls. Without thinking, Andy moved to follow. Minna caught her by the arm.

"Don'tcha go chasin' that cat out there." Minna's amber eyes were eerily bright.

Inexplicably, Andy shivered. "Why?"

"Mine shafts aplenty all over them knolls. Lots of soft spots in the earth. People has dropped into 'em and been hurt bad, even killed." Minna grimaced. "Rattlers nest in some of them old shafts."

Andy shook herself. What was she thinking—chasing after a cat? With Jack's and her lives on the line, she dare not let herself get sidetracked. If she couldn't get her mind to release the secret of Nightmare Man's identity—then she'd attack from another angle. Knowledge was power, and right now it seemed the only weapon Jack and she might wield against their nemesis.

In the motel office she called Information, obtained the phone number for the company whose name was printed on the back of the glossy print, and dialed.

Suppose this was yet another dead end? With trembling fingers and pinching stomach she stared down at the print of the man and woman standing in front of the same assay office where her father had had his picture taken over twenty years ago. No. If her thief had seen *this* print, it would also be missing.

A youthful, high-pitched, feminine voice answered on the second ring. "Western Vistas."

Barely curbing her anxiety, Andy introduced herself, stating research for the new book as her reason for calling. "Is Western Vistas a wholesale distributor?"

"We are."

"Where do you get your photographs?"

"Where?" The high voice whined with puzzlement.

"Yes." Andy fidgeted impatiently as Minna strode into the office. "Who do you buy them from?"

"We don't buy them from anyone." The woman laughed— apparently at herself. "I'm sorry. Don't know where my head is today. We take the photos ourselves, develop them ourselves and distribute them ourselves."

"Oh." Despite warning herself to the contrary, Andy felt hope building. "I'm interested in some pictures taken of an assay office that once occupied the site presently occupied by the Golden Broom Hotel in Alder Gulch. Would it be possible to speak to whoever shot those photographs?"

"Sure. Give me the ID number."

Andy found the number on the back of the print.

"Hang on a minute." There was a noisy clank as the woman apparently dropped the phone on the desk. Andy heard some rustling noises in the background and a radio playing the latest Clint Black hit. With her patience thinning, she scooted one hip onto the edge of Minna's orderly desk, absently noting how surprisingly tidy the whole office was, what with all the cats who had run of the place. From another room the washing machine vibrated loudly. Off balance. Like her.

"You still there?"

"Yes." Her heart leapt into her throat.

"Wouldn't you know this is the one print we distribute that we didn't produce. We—well, you don't want to know how we did it. Suffice it to say, the people in the photo were old friends of my in-laws, so, for the fun of it, my husband included it in our line. But the truth is, it was taken way before our time."

Andy gripped the receiver so hard her fingers ached. "Would you know who shot the original?"

"No. My husband might, but he's on a road shoot in Arizona."

A sinking feeling plunged through Andy, dragging her hope with it. "When do you expect him?"

"Not for another week. If you'd like to leave a number?"

"That's all right." Andy noticed Minna had left again. She could hear her talking to someone in the apartment behind the office. One of her cats? A visitor? Another phone? Andy couldn't tell. "I'll try again later."

"Say," the woman said, reclaiming Andy's attention, "there's a guy in Alder Gulch who might help you. He's one of our biggest customers. Virgil Cooper. He used to take scenic photographs, but as the town was restored the demand started overweighing his development facilities and he contracted with us. Maybe he can answer some of your questions."

"Thanks. I'll try him." Shaken, Andy hung up, blinking at this new twist of events. Had Coop photographed her father in front of the assay office all those years ago? She wanted

o scream with frustration. Instead, she swore. Why hadn't
she shown her photo to him? As if reliving the moment, she
remembered the odd sensation that had kept her from doing
so. What did it mean? Was her subconscious warning her that
Virgil Cooper was Nightmare Man?

It didn't matter. That possibility wouldn't stop her. Nor was
she waiting until Jack was off work. She was going to see
Coop now. Her gaze flicked to the glossy print in her unsteady
grip. Her photograph might be gone, but she still had this one.

Minna appeared in the doorway, holding two mugs. A nut-
meg-and-cinnamon scent reached her. "Ya looked like ya
could use a cuppa tea."

Andy smiled at the woman, grateful for the thoughtfulness.
But she hated tea. "Maybe later, okay? Right now I have to
see Virgil Cooper."

"Surely you kin spare a minute for some apple spiced? It'll
warm yer insides."

"I really appreciate your kindness, but, well…" Andy hes-
tated. Every time she told someone she didn't like tea, they
always insisted she'd like *this* one, *it* didn't taste like tea. No
one seemed to understand that *she* could detect the "tea" taste
in all teas and that was what she disliked. She didn't want to
seem ungracious, but she was in a hurry. "I'm not a tea
drinker."

"That's what I git fer assumin'. I'll fix ya some coffee,
then. Jest take a jiff." Minna wheeled for the hallway.

"Later, please?"

Minna glanced over her shoulder. Disappointment shone in
her amber eyes and there was an odd pink tinge to her flat
cheeks, but she nodded. "Okey-doke."

Andy hurried outside, her mind embroiled in a war of questions. Why had Coop acted as if he didn't know where the
glossy prints he sold were produced, when he knew perfectly
well? Did he actually sell any prints from Taiwan? Or had it
merely been an offhand remark?

On Main Street she saw Jack emerge from the bank. He pulse quickened at the sight of him, and she realized she wa in danger of losing not only her life in this town, but he heart, as well. *Oh, Gram, what am I doing? Tim deserve better from me.*

Jack raced for his Appaloosa. The shoot-out was second away. The air smelled damp and clean. Forcing her mind of Jack and back to the matter at hand, she darted across the street. The first round of gunfire began as her footsteps clat tered on the wooden sidewalk.

Jack caught sight of her when he reined the Appaloos toward the center of town. As their gazes locked, Andy' breath snagged and a smile sprang to her lips. Even at thi distance she could read the worry in Jack's gray-green eyes Squaring her shoulders, she broke eye contact and headed fo the photo shop.

Through the window of the door she saw Coop behind the counter. The bell jangled overhead as she entered, and the slight stench of ammonia teased her nose.

Andy strode to the counter. Outside the gunfight was in fu swing. "Hello, Mr. Cooper."

Coop looked up. His dark eyes narrowed behind his roun glasses. As yesterday, he wore his riverboat gambler attire "Ms. Hart, isn't it?"

"Yes." She laid the print on the counter.

He glanced down at it, then up at her, bafflement and un easiness now swimming in his dark eyes. "Where'd you ge this?"

Andy opened her mouth to speak. Behind her, glass shat tered. Reflexively, she jerked toward the sound. Something zinged past the tip of her nose. The window in the door hac exploded. Jagged pieces of glass rained on the floor. Shock slammed through Andy, turning her limbs leaden, her minc mushy. As if in slow motion, she gazed back at Coop.

He looked surprised. Andy tried to speak, but the red stair

lossoming on his shirtfront captured her attention. She glanced up in time to see his eyes glaze. Then Coop crumpled to the floor behind the counter.

Andy's scream died on her tongue as the bell over the door tinkled and the sound of footsteps crunching glass knifed through her shock. Ducking reflexively, she scrambled around the edge of the counter as a man advanced into the shop, his gun barrel pointed directly at her.

Chapter Eight

"Andy, what the hell is going on in here?" Jack holstered his gun and hurried to her. Catching her gently yet firmly by her upper arms, he pulled her to her feet. She was deadweight slumping against him. Jack glanced over her head, seeing for the first time the man sprawled behind the counter.

Something icy touched his heart.

Andy lifted her head, her dark hair falling across her shoulders. Her eyes were distant as if she were seeing it all again. "The door. The glass. Exploded. Coop. Oh, God, he needs help." Strength seemed to return to her then. She shoved against Jack's chest, righting herself. "We have to get a doctor, an ambulance."

"I'll take care of that. Right now I want you to sit down." Jack guided her to the bench that Coop used for posing his clients.

"I'm all right, Jack." She sat on the edge, anxiously twining her fingers. "Please, help Coop."

He rushed back around the counter. Coop's eyes were wide open, but Jack feared the only thing he was seeing was the bright light of heaven beckoning. Jack dropped to his knees and felt for a pulse. None. He removed his jacket and covered Coop's face.

With his nerves jumping and his mouth dry, Jack returned to Andy. Her eyes were full of hope. He shook his head. Al-

color drained from her face. He sat beside her and drew her into his arms.

She leaned against him, but was so still, he suspected she was numb with shock. Dear God, what was going on? She'd promised to stay put in her cabin until he came for her after the noon performance. Something pretty serious must have made her disregard that promise. She understood the dangers. "What were you doing here?"

"What in the—!" The outcry came from the doorway, suspending Andy's reply.

Jack jerked his head up.

Gene Mott had his electric wheelchair poised at the threshold. His eerily pale eyes were wide with dismay. "Somebody throw a rock through the window?"

"I'm afraid it's worse than that." Jack rose, stepping protectively in front of Andy as he moved toward the door. Glass crunched beneath his feet. "Don't come in."

Red Yager and Duke Plummer appeared behind Gene. Plummer said, "Why shouldn't we?"

"Go call the sheriff, Yager. Virgil Cooper's been shot dead."

Duke Plummer blinked as if Jack had slapped him. Red Yager reared back in astonishment. But Jack couldn't tell whether their shocked reactions were real or faked.

In contrast, Gene Mott's face was stony with disbelief. His fingers curled around the gearshift of his electric wheelchair. "Outta my way, Jack. I'll see for myself."

"I said, stay out. This is a crime scene."

Gene's eyes narrowed and crimson climbed his neck, but his grip eased off the control, and he breathed deeply as if trying to curb his anger. Jack didn't have time to worry about Gene's temper getting out of control. He glanced again at Red. "Now, Yager."

Red's head bobbed and his mustache twitched as he nodded vigorously. "Of course, of course."

He wheeled around and hastened down the boardwalk toward his hotel. Jack eyed Duke and Gene. "You two stay put and don't let anyone in here until the sheriff arrives. I'm taking Ms. Hart back to her cabin at the Motherlode Motel. The sheriff can question her there."

Jack disliked leaving the crime scene in the hands of three of his suspects, but he liked less the idea of Andy sitting there with Virgil Cooper's dead body until the sheriff showed up.

Minna Kroft was stepping onto the porch of the motel office as they emerged from the path. She was pink cheeked and a bit breathless, as if she'd been running.

"Whatever is goin' on?" she asked, before Jack could say anything. "You two look plumb odd."

With his arm around Andy's waist, Jack told Minna the news.

Minna blanched, then recovered quickly, her face radiating concern as she hurried up to them. "You poor thing. No wonder yer white as snow." She grasped Andy by both hands. "You come right on in here and let me fix ya some coffee."

Before Jack could stop Minna, she dragged Andy from his side and guided her through the motel office to the personal quarters in the back. Dismayed, Jack followed.

He couldn't forget Minna stomping the scorpion to death, or his niggling suspicions of her, but her voice rang with the same genuine regard for Andy that he'd often heard in his mother's voice when she comforted a friend in distress. Was she the world's greatest actress? Or had he misjudged this woman? Actually thought she might be Nightmare Man? Chagrined at himself, he said, "I think tea would be better."

Minna's kitchen was a large, small-windowed room dominated by an antique oak dining set with mismatched chairs and blue-and-white-checked cushions. Minna shook her head. "She don't like tea. But some spirits'd fix her up right quick. Bring some color back into those cheeks and take off the chill that's icin' her innards."

"That's a good idea," Jack agreed, feeling more comfortable about his growing belief that Minna Kroft was exactly what she appeared to be: a kindly, middle-aged woman.

"Take her on into the livin' room, whilst I fetch the brandy bottle from the cellar."

The compact living room was extremely tidy, and although it lacked knickknacks and family photographs, there was a built-in bookcase where some kind of trophies shared shelf space with an array of colorful paperbacks. The furniture, old and mismatched, looked comfortable, a perception enhanced by the big Persian sprawled proprietarily on the middle cushion of the sofa.

Jack led Andy to the sofa. Her face was pale. Settling on an end cushion next to the big cat, she curled her legs beneath her, and reached out and stroked the animal's head.

Jack sat on the other end, separated from Andy by the purring cat. He rubbed his fingers down its soft back, inadvertently brushing Andy's fingers. His gaze sought hers, and he was relieved to see the glassiness had left her eyes. The shock was wearing off. "What were you doing at Coop's? You promised you wouldn't leave your cabin, so I'm assuming it must've been important."

She told Jack about discovering that her special photograph was missing, about learning that Virgil Cooper had probably been the one who'd photographed her father in front of the assay office. "I had to see if he knew something."

He could shake Andy for the danger she'd placed herself in by going to Coop's alone. And yet, he knew he'd do the same under the same circumstances. Despite the foolhardiness of her actions, he admired her spirit. Besides, he hadn't thought Nightmare Man would try anything this bold in broad daylight. "Do you think Coop was killed because he knew something about your parents' murders?"

"I don't know." Was that why Virgil was dead? Or had

someone tried to kill her? "I'm not so sure the bullet wasn't meant for me."

A chill plunged through Jack. "I think you'd better explain that."

Minna arrived and pressed a cup of brandy into Andy's hands. "Drink, girl."

Andy took a swallow and felt a sudden rush of strength from the bracing heat of the liquor. Jack was still waiting for an answer, his scowl marking his impatience. She sat straighter. "If the sound of breaking glass hadn't startled me. If I hadn't lurched away when I turned, the bullet would have struck me squarely in the back of the head."

Minna gasped.

Jack swore under his breath. He wanted to pull Andy into his arms, but not in front of Minna. There would already be enough gossip around town about them, after his insistence on getting her away from the crime scene. He shoved to his feet.

The telephone rang in the outer office. Minna excused herself and hurried off.

"Maybe that's the sheriff." Jack followed Minna across the room. Stopping at the doorway, he spun back, cast Andy a troubled look, ran a hand through his thick black hair, then glanced away. As he paced, his gaze swung across the trophies on the bookcase, and absently he noted they'd been awarded to Minna for her marksmanship with a rifle.

Andy watched Jack pace as she caressed the cat's underbelly with her free hand. There was something comforting about the Persian's presence, and she was grateful her throat no longer constricted as it had when she'd first arrived, grateful her restored memory had abolished her fear of cats.

It dawned on her that the shock was receding. Her anger returning. She was alive to fight another day. But poor Jack probably thought she'd slipped off the deep end, leaving him to face Nightmare Man alone.

Setting her cup on the end table, she rose and crossed the room to him. "I'm all right, so, whatever else, don't waste your time worrying about me."

Jack reached down and stroked his knuckles along her chin, his touch so gentle, it sent shivers of awareness to her toes. He swallowed, but didn't speak. His silvery green eyes showed a momentary spark of pain she could not account for, but she could not have misread the desire in their depths. She thought he might kiss her and, remembering the feel of his mouth on hers, she wished he would.

He leaned closer.

"Telephone's fer you, Andy," Minna interrupted, shattering the mood. "A Mr. Frettin'."

Tim! A hot shaft of guilt knifed through Andy. "Freyton." She corrected Minna in a muttered breath and cast a flustered glance at Jack.

"Ya have ta use the phone in the office."

With a blush heating her cheeks, Andy nodded and left the room, but she didn't hurry toward the office. She wasn't ready to talk to Tim about all that had been occurring. She grimaced, holding back a scream of frustration. *So, what am I going to say, Gram? Oh, Tim, you won't believe all that's happened— I'm having the most wonderful time in Montana?*

Andy stopped and drew a deep breath, shaking off the last vestiges of shock. This wasn't some Club Med vacation. Her life was on the line—physically and emotionally. She needed to deal with it. Tim deserved the truth. All of it.

In case she didn't survive.

Half an hour later Andy said goodbye and replaced the receiver. She swiped at the tear spilling down her cheek. It had been the most difficult conversation she'd had with anyone in a long while, and Tim had exhibited more emotion than he'd done the whole ten years she'd known him. Surprisingly more. He'd wanted to send in the marines to rescue Jack and her, but she'd finally made him see that that would give them only a momentary reprieve, when what was needed was a permanent solution.

In the kitchen Andy startled Minna. She jumped, then, looking flustered, her face quickly growing red, started toward Andy. "Well, now, I reckon I got some paperwork needs seein' to."

As Minna hustled past her into the hallway that led to the office, Andy wondered if she'd been eavesdropping on Jack and whomever he was talking to in the living room. Her stomach knotted. She couldn't blame Minna for being curious. Even if her curiosity was of the ghoulish sort. After all, someone she'd known for years had been killed.

Andy strode into the living room. Jack was talking to a man in uniform, whose back was to her. The man continued talking until Jack glanced her way. Then he shifted around. If Jack was a grizzly, this man was a leopard, sleek and lean, his tawny hair clipped close to his head over small, flat ears.

His uniform consisted of a dark brown shirt with light brown tabs at the shoulders, light brown slacks with dark brown stripes down the legs, a dark brown, billed cap and black, police-issue boots. A deadly-looking gun rode his hip, and his shirt sported a seven-point star bearing the Montana state seal and the insignia patch of the Madison County Sheriff's Department.

She guessed his age around forty-five. His face was as tight as a leopard's, with a similar keenness in his hazel eyes that told Andy this was not a man to underestimate.

She felt Jack's solicitous gaze on her, but he needn't worry. As long as she had a breath in her body, she would remember who Nightmare Man was. She'd decided to consider it just another deadline she had to meet. And she'd never missed a deadline yet. *Have I, Gram?*

Jack searched her face. She looked different. Somehow calmer. More determined. Jack didn't know what she and her fiancé had discussed for the past half hour, but apparently it had wrought some kind of change in her. Tim Freyton wasn't just a lucky guy, he must also be a hell of a good one. Jack's heart felt like an anvil inside his chest. "Andrea Hart, Sheriff Birdsill."

Andy squared her shoulders and strode across the room, her hand outstretched. "Nice to make your acquaintance, Sheriff, although I could have wished for happier circumstances."

The sheriff nodded, then gestured toward the sofa. "I'll need a statement, Ms. Hart."

Holding her ground, she glanced questioningly at Jack. How much had he told the sheriff? Jack shook his head. Her hands dampened. She'd just told Tim everything, and now it looked as if she'd be telling it again. But not here. Not within Minna's earshot. They couldn't risk the whole town knowing. "Sheriff Birdsill, Mr. Black and I have a rather interesting story concerning the murder of Mr. Cooper, but I'd rather tell you somewhere less...public...say, my cabin."

The sheriff agreed and minutes later they were seated at the dinette table in her cabin.

"What makes you so sure it was murder?" Sheriff Birdsill flicked the brim of his cap, knocking it higher on his forehead, then flipped open the cover of his notepad. "Could have been a ricochet."

"Impossible." Jack shook his head adamantly. "The players use blanks."

The sheriff sighed. "Sometimes live ammo slips through. I can't stress the importance of checking every single round before it's loaded. But human nature being what it is... Well, ole Virgil Cooper might just have been a victim of somebody's carelessness."

"It's more likely his death was deliberate," Andy said. They told him the whole story, up to and including Jack's real name.

"It's an interesting theory, Ms. Hart, er, Woodworth, but

the truth is, at this point you don't have any real proof that someone is after you. I would, however, caution you to keep an eye open. I remember your parents' case. I'd only been with the department six months and we don't get many double homicides. I'd love to close it off the books, but unless you can give me a name to start with, there isn't much I can do."

He closed his notepad and stood.

Jack rose also. "Surely you're not writing this off as an accident?"

"I never jump to conclusions." Birdsill tugged his hat back down his forehead. "Right now I'm just compiling information, and you've given me plenty to chew on."

"Do you have any idea what kind of gun was used?" Jack pressed, the reporter in him surfacing.

"You know I'm not at liberty to answer such a question, Mr. Starett." The sheriff strode to the door, then looked back over his shoulder. "But judging by the exit wound, I have a pretty good idea."

Andy shoved up and out of her chair. She felt a twinge of hope rising in her. "How long before you know for certain?"

"Can't say. First we have to retrieve the bullet, then run it through a battery of tests. But eventually, we'll discover whose gun it was fired from." He opened the door. "Meanwhile, I have to ask you two not to leave the county without telling me. So, be extra cautious."

NIGHTMARE MAN GROWLED aloud. Two hours since he'd swallowed three super-strength Tylenol and still the ache at his temples throbbed unrelentingly. Stress. Even the muscles in his neck felt twisted like barbed wire.

Damn that Lee Lee Woodworth! Coop was dead because of her. If she'd died like she was supposed to twenty years ago, it wouldn't have been necessary to try such a bold move today. Cruel, cruel fate! If the glass hadn't deflected the bullet... If she hadn't reacted so quickly...

But Lee Lee had proven years ago that she had more lives than a cat.

He pulled the photo album from its secret hiding place behind the bookcase and carried it to the kitchen table. As before, stale paper smell rose from the album the second he flipped it open. Gingerly, he turned the yellow pages, stopping at last at an aged photograph of himself standing before the old assay office that was now the Golden Broom Hotel. The face was thinner, younger, but recognizable as his own. Coop had taken this picture.

And Arlo's.

He supposed it was just as well that Coop was dead. He might have told her of this photograph.

Nightmare Man drew the photograph he'd stolen from Andy's cabin out of his jacket pocket and laid it next to his picture.

Arlo had looked this same way the night of his death. Shaking his head, Nightmare Man taped the edges of the photograph to the yellowed page. He hadn't wanted to kill Arlo, but when he'd come home unexpectedly and seen poor Marcy.... *If only Arlo hadn't started yelling, if only I hadn't lost my temper.* But he had lost his temper, the rage a crimson sheet descending over his eyes, blinding him to everything.

And afterward, the child had seen. Seen him. Could tell someone.

He glanced down at the newly acquired photograph. Too bad he didn't have a photograph of Coop. It seemed only fitting that he should be remembered like the others. He turned another page, his fingertips slipping gently over each face that stared up at him from the album. Arlo, Jack Starett, Sr., and his own beloved Marcy.

No, he hadn't wanted to kill Coop, either. But self-preservation drove him and he'd risked exposure today in order to protect himself. Sheriff Birdsill was no fool. He'd soon declare Coop's death a murder. There'd be no question of that when he realized the bullet was gone. Taken. Dug out of the wall behind Coop's counter.

The bullet felt smooth and cool between his forefinger and thumb. Without it, the police could never trace a path to his gun, and since he hadn't wanted to kill Coop, there was no evidence, circumstantial or otherwise, pointing to him. In all likelihood, no one would ever be charged with the crime.

A smile teetered at the corners of his mouth and the ache in his temples seemed to snap away as he taped the bullet to an empty section of the page where Virgil Cooper's picture should have been.

Returning the album to its hiding place, he settled in his chair and put his mind to the matter of Lee Lee Woodworth, alias Andrea Hart. Just thinking about her brought a red haze hovering at the edges of his vision. Before now, that was all he had feared. The crimson haze. His anger.

But *she* had him plotting. Plotting her murder. He shuddered, feeling dirtied by these thoughts. He hadn't meant to kill the others. Didn't remember the actual acts of murder. But he couldn't say that anymore. Not after today. Not after Coop.

He could still feel the smooth trigger under his finger, smell the cordite burning his nostrils, hear the explosion of the fired gun. It didn't matter that it wasn't Coop he'd been after. He'd killed him just the same. A nerve jumped in his jaw.

What worried him was the fact that he hadn't been angry when he'd pulled the trigger. Just scared. Of discovery. If Lee Lee remembered...his life would be over. He drew himself straighter in the chair, clamping his teeth in determination. She would be dead before it came to that.

Chapter Nine

"Damn! Why can't I remember who Nightmare Man is?" Andy slammed her fist on the table.

Her outburst jarred Jack's ragged nerves. The sheriff had departed three hours earlier, after which they'd sat at her table drinking coffee and discussing every aspect and angle they recalled preceding the shooting—hoping against hope someone or something they'd seen would help them figure out who'd killed Coop. They'd wiped out one and a half pots of Seattle's Best Coffee, but had come up with zilch.

Jack could see that Andy was on the verge of collapse. She needed time out from the gut-knotting tension of their situation; she needed a good night's rest, one free from the fear of being killed in her sleep.

He shoved back his chair and stood. "You've been through enough in the past twenty-four hours to do in two people. Grab some things for overnight. We're going to Butte."

"But the sheriff said—"

"I'll let Birdsill know."

Could they really just run away for the night? *What do you think, Gram, can we?* A little voice in her head, sounding familiarly like Gram's, answered, *Of course you can. Nightmare Man isn't likely to push his luck and try something this soon after Virgil Cooper's death. Not with the sheriff and his deputies in town.* Andy smiled. The prospect of spending a

stress-free night somewhere—with Jack—lightened her spirits, eased the strain in her shoulders and the kinks in her
stomach.

"All right. Let's do it." While she packed her suitcase with
the bare essentials, Jack hurried out to use Minna's phone.
By the time he'd returned, Andy was ready.

They stopped at his cabin for his clothes, then ran through
the rain to the parking lot and into her Cherokee. Jack drove,
repeatedly checking the rearview mirror for headlights.

"Are we being followed?" Andy's voice had an uneasy
lilt.

Again Jack checked the mirror. It remained dark. *Which
meant nothing.* But there was no need worrying Andy any
further. "Doesn't look like it."

Every nerve in his body felt frazzled.

Half an hour down the road a sudden flicker of light reflected in the rearview mirror. Headlights. Way back. Slowly
the beams of light grew larger as the vehicle behind gained
on them. It was two car lengths back when Jack swung left
onto the freeway ramp.

Seconds later its lights reappeared in the mirror as it sped
up the ramp behind the Cherokee.

Once on Interstate 90, Jack was assailed with myriad vehicles' headlights glaring at him from the mirror. There was
no way of knowing if they were being followed now. He
tossed a quick look at Andy. Her hands were clenched in her
lap and her eyes were fixed on a spot straight ahead. He
checked the mirror again. Was he being paranoid? Or was
Nightmare Man in one of the cars behind them?

The possibility chilled Jack, and he took a deliberately
roundabout way through downtown Butte until he felt certain
it was safe to proceed to the hotel he'd decided on, a security-
conscious establishment.

Glad to be out of the confines of the Cherokee, Andy
rushed to help Jack with the luggage. Their hands bumped as

she reached for her overnighter. Jack flinched as if she'd burned him. For half a second his gaze met hers, then a flustered expression sprang into his silvery green eyes and he yanked their bags from the trunk and stepped away. "Lock the hatch."

As Andy followed Jack into the hotel lobby her energy seemed to drain like water from an emptying sink. She was aware of a bone tiredness so deep she barely retained the physical strength to hold herself upright.

He asked the registrar for adjoining rooms.

The thought of being alone all night in a hotel room terrified Andy. She tugged on his coat sleeve.

"Jack, I don't think I can stand sleeping alone tonight," she whispered. "Please, make it a double room?"

Jack's heart leapt into his throat, and he had a hell of a time swallowing over it. He knew her invitation wasn't for sex, but, curse all, didn't she realize sharing a bedroom with her drove him crazy? Somehow he kept his voice level. "We've changed our minds. We'd like a double room."

He had no chance of enlightening Andy on the subject of her effect on him. She fell asleep seconds after climbing into bed, leaving Jack stretched out on his own bed, staring at the ceiling, fighting the ache to climb in beside her, to hold her as he had the night before, to press her ripe curves against him—and so much more.

Thunder rumbled in the distance, and he jammed his pillow with his fist. Andy was not only vulnerable, but engaged to another man; he had to quit coveting her. He ground his teeth in frustration, taking back every kind thing he'd thought about Tim Freyton, wanting to wring his neck for not rushing here to protect her. What kind of a jerk was he, anyway?

Clinging to his anger, Jack concentrated on staying alert to sounds of danger. Instead, he became entangled in the whisper of Andy's breathing, in the enticing fragrance of her delicate perfume.

In the end, exhaustion won out over his warring emotions and pulled him into a deep, dreamless sleep. In the morning, he had to admit, he felt revitalized, better than he had in days.

But their reprieve was over.

He called Wally and brought him up to speed. Then once again they were in the Cherokee, speeding along Interstate 90. A tangible tension clutched Jack as Butte grew more distant in the rearview mirror. He tightened his fingers on the steering wheel. Today might just be the day Andy remembered.

She broke the silence. "What did Wally say when you told him about Coop?"

Jack glanced over at her. She wore red Tony Lamas, faded jeans and a lightweight, blue denim shirt. Her hair was tied at the nape with a red ribbon. Gone were the violet smudges, like delicate bruises, under her intriguingly beautiful eyes, and the tightness on either side of her sweetly kissable mouth. She looked rested…and good enough to eat. God, why did he punish himself like this? "Wally thinks we should pack it in. Not go back to Alder Gulch."

Jack kept to himself Wally's thoughts on "no story being worth their dying for."

Andy sighed. "I take it you explained why we have to go back?"

"Yes." But he respected Wally's judgment, his experience with Nightmare Man. Jack glanced at her again. "I promised him if you couldn't remember within the next couple of days, we'd leave."

Jack braced for an argument, and was surprised when none came.

Instead, she smacked her palms against her thighs. "Why can't I remember?"

Jack bit down his own frustration. As much as he wanted her to remember, he knew wanting it wouldn't make it so. "Suppressed memory is one of those things that returns when it returns. You can't push the river."

"No, but there must be some way I can prod it a little."
She bumped her head back against the headrest and closed
her eyes. They were off the interstate and traveling the road
for Alder Gulch when she opened them. "I have an idea. Let's
visit the spot where my house used to be, where I lived as a
little girl. Maybe that will nudge something loose."

"Okay." Jack had heard of cases where seeing something
familiar could trigger a memory. He gave the sky a cursory
glance. It was cloudless; even the road was dusty dry, as if
yesterday's rainstorm had been a dream. "I like the idea. The
players have canceled all shows for two days while the police
are investigating Cooper's death. We can get an early start
and spend the day if you want."

"Good." The plan of action rallied her spirits, but the day
ahead still daunted. Striving for something to take her mind
off it, she changed the subject. "Why didn't we go to your
family ranch last night?"

The ranch? Jack glanced at her again, imagining his mother
and sister fussing over Andy, wrapping her in the Starett family's cocoon of love. It made a heartwarming picture. A rock
hit the windshield. Startling and sobering him. "My family
won't be putting out the welcome mat for me any time soon,
I'm afraid. At the moment I'm persona non grata."

"Oh?"

"Before I left, Mom and Jonna and Max read me the riot
act for even considering trying to flush out Nightmare Man.
They had reason to hope I was finally getting over my obsession."

He gave a self-deprecating laugh, deliberately making light
of a moment that would go down as one of the worst in his
life. His chest squeezed as he remembered his family standing
united in disapproval. In disappointment. In fear.

The look of pity on Andy's face stirred him on. "Don't
worry, they'll forgive me...eventually."

If I don't end up getting myself killed.

"I envy you your family." She leaned back against the headrest again and stared out at the vast landscape. With every passing mile Alder Gulch loomed closer. Fear teased her, but Andy realized she felt less afraid with Jack near.

Strange. Three days ago, Gram, I couldn't have imagined myself with any man but Tim. Never, ever a man like Jack Starett, Jr. Maybe in my fantasies. But not in reality.

She glanced over at his arresting profile and her breath caught. He was the opposite of Tim in so many ways, obvious ways, subtle ways. Yet, since the first draft of her first historical romance—forever banished to a top shelf of her office closet in Seattle—*he* was the hero she'd written in every book.

But how did Jack feel about her? Should she tell him she'd broken off her engagement with Tim? That it was him she wanted? Or would that merely embarrass them both?

She considered the night before last, the night she'd thrown herself at him. Oh, sure, he'd responded. Passionately. What healthy heterosexual male wouldn't have? But his rejection still stung, and her battered heart ached with the realization that it was quite possible Jack's main interest in her was her ability to bring his father's murderer to justice, to end his own obsession.

He turned and looked at her. Andy blinked and glanced away.

Jack swallowed hard. Although he'd tried reining in the desire that coursed through his veins with every glance in Andy's direction, it resisted control. He felt as skittish as a wild stallion. Deliberately, he focused his attention on the countryside whizzing by, but the ugliness of it stirred a different passion.

If only it was raining, or dark. Anything that would hide the seemingly endless slag piles bordering the road—grotesque reminders of the strip mining that was once so popular in this area of Montana. The practice had gnawed away the rolling hillsides and now blocked from view what remained of the natural beauty.

And this area of Montana *was* beautiful.

The thought gave him an idea. "You did say you could ride a horse, didn't you?"

The rooftops of Alder Gulch appeared ahead. Andy's stomach lurched and she gave Jack a tight smile, thinking it odd that she recalled earlier memories, but couldn't evoke the face of the man who'd killed her parents. "Daddy had me riding at age three."

"And since then?"

"Gram didn't like it much, but all through my teens I spent as much time as possible at her friend Charlie's farm, riding one of his big old geldings. Why?"

The more he thought about it, the more Jack liked his idea. With a horse to concentrate on, Andy would feel less pressured to remember, and on horseback, he knew they'd be more mobile, could—if the need arose—more easily elude any pursuer. "I thought we'd ride out to your old house. Take a picnic lunch."

Andy brightened. "Yeah, why not?"

But her expression took on a false cheeriness as they drove along Main Street. Jack, too, felt tense. He kept his eyes peeled for their suspects, half hoping Nightmare Man would see him with Andy and know the opposition he faced if he wanted her.

Sheriff Birdsill was standing on the porch of Andy's cabin as she and Jack carried their luggage up the rise. The sheriff looked disturbed, even more feral than yesterday. One unhappy leopard. The aroma of fried bacon clung to his clothing. "I hoped you hadn't skipped town."

Jack's pulse picked up a beat. "What's happened, Sheriff?"

Birdsill flicked the bill of his cap with his thumb and forefinger, popping it up and away from his tawny eyebrows.

Aggravation glinted in his eyes. "The bullet that killed Virgil Cooper's been stolen. Dug right out of the wall, probably with a pocketknife. You own a pocketknife, Mr. Starett?"

Jack blanched. "Surely, after what we told you yesterday, you don't believe *I* killed Coop?"

"Right now I suspect everyone. Don't leave town again. Either of you. For any reason. It's real likely you'll be telling me that story of yours a couple more times."

He left them staring at one another.

Andy spoke first. "He can't be serious?"

"Oh, I'd say he's serious, all right. We were alone with the body for several minutes before anyone else came on the scene. Come on." Jack spurred her on to unlock the door, then deposited her suitcase on the bed. The odor of stale coffee grounds hung in the air. He gave the cabin a thorough going-over while Andy fidgeted with something on her desk.

As he came out of the bathroom, he noticed that her face was ashen. "What's wrong?"

She turned toward him, holding a piece of paper by the edge. "This was on my desk."

Jack took the paper from her. It was a computer-printed message. "Hi, Lee Lee. Remember me? I remember you. Did you have fun in Butte last night? Soon we're going to meet face-to-face and talk about old times."

Cold swept through Jack. So, they had been followed, after all. He dropped the note onto the desk. "Don't touch it again. I'll get Birdsill back here. Maybe he can trace it—find out whose printer it came from."

"No, Jack." Andy's voice quavered. "It came from mine."

"What?"

"Yes, I always use a CG Times font, ten point, for printing draft copies of my manuscript. It saves paper. I can't imagine the odds of someone else in this town using it."

Jack crossed the room and pulled her close against him. She let him hold her for a full sixty seconds, then she stepped back, squaring her shoulders, her eyes bright with indignation. "I'm all right."

"You sure?"

"Yes. I'm not going to let him beat us. We have to figure this out."

"Okay." Jack considered what she'd told him about the font. "How about another writer? Maybe Gene Mott uses this same font on his laser printer."

Shaking her head, Andy gave him a look that said she thought he was grasping at straws. "Gene might have a laser printer, and that printer might have this font, but we don't know that he'd use it." She lifted a hank of her hair off her forehead. "Besides, how easily could a man in a wheelchair get into my cabin?"

"Hell, whoever did it had all night to get in and out of here." Jack stormed over to the door. "Now that you mention it, how the blazes *did* someone get in? The door was locked nice and tight when we arrived."

Andy watched him examining the door, her twined fingers clutched to her chest. Her heart thudded against the heels of her hands.

Jack glanced at her. "Whoever got in herè used a key."

A shiver zipped down Andy's spine. The sheriff might have the authority to insist on her remaining in Alder Gulch, but no one could make her spend another night in this cabin. She suppressed the urge to run across the room and enfold herself in Jack's protective embrace, forced herself to concentrate on who could have gotten in. One name rose inside her head in giant neon letters. "Minna?"

"Either that or she let someone else in."

Andy hated thinking she couldn't trust the friendly motel proprietress. "Maybe someone stole the key."

"Could be." Jack's brows dipped toward his eyes.

"Who knew we'd be gone overnight?"

"Plenty of people." As if he'd just realized they could be

overheard, Jack shut the door and strode toward her, his voice lowered as he counted on his fingers. "Minna could have listened to my conversation with Birdsill. Cliff waved at us when we were driving through town last night. Given his mind-set, he would assume we were—"

Jack broke off. A disconcerted expression seized his strong features, giving him an embarrassed-little-boy look. "You know."

Andy made a face. She could guess at the gutters Cliffie's mind rolled through. "And he'd probably tell his uncle."

Jack nodded. "Duke Plummer could have seen us from the museum as we loaded the luggage into the Cherokee. Red Yager could have seen us from the bar as we drove past."

Andy hugged herself. Remembering was getting more crucial by the second, but the wall inside her head protecting her from seeing Nightmare Man's face remained solid.

Jack's big hand landed reassuringly on her shoulder. "Let's see what Minna has to say about this."

Minna wasn't home. A sign saying "Be Back At One O'Clock" hung in the motel office window. Jack tried the office door. It was unlocked, the keys to the cabins right behind the counter for anyone to help themselves. Jack grunted in frustration. "That answers the question of who had access to the cabin keys. The whole town. Now what?"

Andy snapped her fingers as she was struck by an idea. "Duke Plummer. What with all that's been going on, until you mentioned him in connection with the museum, I'd completely put out of my mind the way he reacted the day I showed him my father's photograph. I'm certain he knows something."

"You showed him your dad's photo?" Jack rubbed his jaw. "Why?"

"Because it was in an old family album of his that I found a snapshot of the assay office in my photograph. Of course, that was before I realized the man in my photograph was my father. I asked Duke if he recognized the man and that's when he acted so odd."

An old family album of Duke Plummer's? Jack recalled the book he'd seen Duke holding when he'd come across Gene and him in the church. Was that book the same album Andy was talking about? New suspicions tumbled through his brain, pieces falling into place, stirring hope. Could it be this simple? This obvious? "Red mentioned Duke was a taxidermist. Surely that includes birds."

Reflexively, Andy touched her left wrist. "With three giant talons?"

Jack caught her elbow and they began walking toward the museum. "A condor, maybe?"

An image of that ugly bird, a member of the vulture family, sprang to mind. Andy's stomach knotted and she knew instinctively Jack was right. If the scar on her wrist was made by a bird's claw, the bird would have to have talons as large as a falcon or a condor. "I thought all condors were protected—on endangered species lists."

Jack shrugged. "I'm no expert on condors. I know the California condors are protected, but that's only been since the late eighties. You were scarred over twenty years ago."

Andy saw his point. "But how would Duke or anyone else acquire such a gruesome souvenir?"

The sun beat against Jack's shoulder blades, spreading an uncomfortable warmth through him as they crossed Main Street and headed up the walk to the museum. "Duke spends every winter traveling across the country on his Harley. He might have come by one in the wilderness, or even bought one off some two-bit tourist attraction—presuming he's our man."

"If he's not, then how would one of our other suspects have laid their hands on the kind of bird claw we're talking about?"

Remembering the scorpion, Jack said, "Duke's pretty generous with his gifts. Assuming he even secured said item, he could very well have given it away."

"You don't sound too convinced that Duke Plummer is Nightmare Man."

"To paraphrase Birdsill, I'm not ruling anyone out yet." Jack stopped. "Looks like the museum is closed, too."

Andy glanced behind them. The morning was rapidly growing hotter. The air seemed heavy, oppressive. The kind of day when tempers flared and emotions raged out of control. She shook off the foreboding creeping over her.

She hadn't noticed before, but Main Street boasted little foot traffic and no vehicles, as if it was deserted, a genuine ghost town. "I suppose the police investigation squelched the tourist trade for the day?"

"Probably." Jack also seemed to sense the odd quietude. Scowling, he gazed up and down the street, then glanced at Andy. "What do you want to do? It's your call."

"I want to talk to Duke Plummer."

Jack spun on his heel and guided her back down the walk. "Plummer lives up the hill, two or three blocks off Main Street. It's more likely we'll find what we're looking for at his house than in this dusty old museum."

Andy agreed. But as they left the dark-windowed museum behind, she felt the skin-prickling sensation of being watched.

Chapter Ten

Duke Plummer lived two short streets up the hill above Main Street. His house, an old, single-story clapboard, had once been a healthy-grass green with snow white trim, but the colors were faded, the paint blistered and chipped. From the home's wraparound porch Andy could see the roof of the Golden Broom and, across the gulch, the Motherlode Motel.

Jack rapped on the door, waited ten seconds and rapped again. Silence answered.

He peered into the nearest window. It was dark and gloomy and definitely not a place Jack would feel at home. He said sarcastically, "Cozy."

Andy moved beside him, cupped her hands over her eyes and peered in. The furniture consisted of one armchair, an ottoman and an end table. Instead of a living room, it looked more like a gruesome wildlife sanctuary for the dead fish and fowl that were mounted on the walls, an inhumane graveyard for the glassy-eyed fox posed on the hearth and the grizzly-bear rug sprawled nearby. Andy grimaced and pulled her gaze sideways. Two yellow eyes caught her attention and she realized she was staring at an owl.

A hoot owl.

Every muscle in her body tensed as a memory flashed through her mind. She was five again, awakened by a loud screech. A hoot owl? No. A scream. A woman's scream.

Mommy's scream.

Heat flushed Andy's body, instantly followed by a chill, leaving her skin clammy, her stomach unsettled. She stumbled back from the window.

Jack caught her arm. "What's wrong?"

She gazed up at him, her eyes clearing, the vision fading. She related the memory to Jack, then with a shaky voice told him, "Jack, I recalled something else, too. One of my parents' friends used to carry a bird claw on his key ring. A large bird claw. He used to brag, 'A big man needs a big talon.'"

Jack's brows lifted. "Aside from the sexual innuendo— does that memory recall anything else for you? A face? A voice?"

Frowning, Andy took a step back and shook her head.

Jack leaned his hip against the window frame and crossed his boots at the ankle. "Was the man big—like me?"

As near as Andy could tell, Jack was a big man in every sense of the word, physically and spiritually, but she supposed he was asking about Nightmare Man's appearance. She squeezed her eyes shut, willing a memory, but it was no use. She sighed. "I was five years old. Everyone was big to me then."

"The question is—what did 'big' mean to *him?*" Jack rubbed his jaw. "Fat?"

"No...somehow that doesn't feel right, but 'big' could refer to height." Andy spoke more softly, conscious that they were outdoors and that their voices might carry. "Like Duke Plummer."

Jack nodded, also speaking more quietly. "But Plummer isn't our only tall suspect. Just because he's now in a wheelchair, don't forget Gene Mott is well over six feet. And he's 'big' in another way, in the famous meaning of the word."

She sighed as it occurred to her there was yet another way "big" could be defined. "As Red Yager is a big man in a small town?"

Noting her frustration, Jack gave her a warm smile. "You'll remember. Consider this progress. It confirms yet again that we're on the right track—and that your memory is returning. Let's check around back."

They followed the porch to the back door and peered in the window. "Look," Jack said. "He has a computer."

Andy peeked into the window. "And a laser printer."

"So, he definitely knows how to use them." Jack knocked again. Apparently Duke Plummer was out.

She glanced toward a garage built against the hillside. It sported the same color scheme as the house. "Do you suppose he's in there?"

Jack shrugged, then scrambled down the porch steps and across a lumpy patch of sun-browned lawn, calling out, "Plummer?"

When there was no response, Jack yanked open the weathered doors that were hinged at the side edges. Daylight poked through the opening, highlighting dust motes and offering the only illumination into the dark recesses of the building. a huge motorcycle nestled in one corner. "Well, he isn't off on his 'hog' somewhere. So he's probably in town."

"This is obviously his workshop." Andy glanced at the plywood slab perched on twin sawhorses in the center of the garage, then at the cluttered metal shelves against one side wall. A dank, musty odor clung to the interior, evoking unpleasant images of the labors performed within.

A tanned animal hide was stretched on the makeshift, plywood worktable, but Andy was more curious about the shelves. She strode closer and inspected their contents, spying spools of thread, needles, animal skulls, antlers, bird feathers, a mason jar filled with teeth, and an old, felt-lined coffee can full of glass eyes. She wrinkled her nose in distaste and despite the warm day, gooseflesh sprang up on her arms and legs.

Jack was right behind her. She started to turn toward him,

but her gaze landed on something perched on the edge of the lowest shelf. The hair on the nape of her neck rose. She leapt back and yelped in terror. "Scorpion."

Jack grabbed her from behind, reflexively pulling her back against the length of his body, pulling her away from the shelves, away from the danger. She felt the wind being sucked from her lungs as his arm tightened around her rib cage. His breath beat hot against her neck and her cheek.

Andy kept her gaze riveted on the scorpion, her pulse roaring in her ears like an ocean wave, her every nerve poised for the attack. The creature stayed as if frozen in place; not even its curled tail twitched. She let out a captured breath and struggled to find her voice, to tell Jack what had only then registered. "It isn't alive."

Jack reacted much more slowly to this news than he had to her cry of terror, relaxing his muscles just enough to spin her around so he could see her face and judge for himself that she was all right. But the moment her ripe curves brushed against him, he was lost, lost in the feel of her, lost in the wonderful smell of her clean hair, lost in the invitation in her beautiful eyes.

He tugged her closer and lowered his mouth to her slightly parted one, then boldly dipped his tongue inside for a real taste of her. She melted against him, feeling so good he could not control the speed of his body's blood-pulsing reaction. He knew she could feel his desire for her, knew he shouldn't feel this way about this woman, but, God help him, he couldn't help himself.

"Aha, I was right," Cliff Mott said on a chuckle.

Andy and Jack jerked apart. Andy's face burned, but Jack looked furious, and she suspected he was wondering the same thing she was: how long had Cliff been standing there? Watching? She realized her first impression of this man was holding steady at every turn.

"What were you right about, Cliff?" Jack asked between clenched teeth.

Cliff seemed oblivious to the hostility emanating from Jack's eyes, from his fisted hands and his hunched shoulders. "About the two of you. But it seems to me you could find a better place to make out."

"We were looking for Duke." Andy stepped between the two men. "Would you know where we could find him, Cliff?"

He tossed his head, flipped a hank of his white blond hair off his forehead and winked at her. He reminded Andy of a white rat she'd had as a child; it, too, had had those small blue eyes.

Cliff said, "Duke and Uncle Gene are out riding. They go about twice a week."

Jack's hostility faltered. "Your uncle rides a horse?"

"Sure. He needs help into the saddle, but once there, he's in full control." His gaze swept Andy and she squirmed uncomfortably. "Say, why don't you come down to the house? Least I can do is offer you something to cool off...on this hot day."

Jack wanted to smash the man's rude innuendo down his throat. With an effort of will he reined in his temper and, instead, placed a protective hand on Andy's shoulder. "That's real neighborly of you, Cliff, but Ms. Hart and I have plans and we need to get started before the day slips any further away."

Cliff's smirk was obnoxious and knowing.

Andy decided he could think whatever he liked. She squared her shoulders and strode past him, but as she started through the doorway, she spotted a string of bird claws—like a line of caught fish—hanging on the side wall. Her step faltered and her stomach clenched. She stifled the urge to point the cord out to Jack, and the stronger urge to yank it from the nail hanger, knowing that it would make noise—and draw Cliff's unwanted attention. Unwanted questions.

It was bad enough that he'd tell his uncle about catching Jack and her in this garage. That Gene would likely tell Duke. What if one of them was Nightmare Man?

She swallowed hard over the unpleasant thought, and the moment Jack and she were alone, heading down the sloping road to Main Street, Andy told him about the cord of bird claws. He seemed only mildly interested. "Trouble is, it doesn't prove Plummer's a killer, just a taxidermist."

Frustration knotted in her chest. She stepped closer to Jack, seeking the reassurance his nearness always induced, but instead of reassurance she sensed a remoteness about him. This was not the same man who'd kissed her a while ago. This was a man holding himself apart from her—and Andy supposed she knew why.

"Jack, I've been meaning to tell you something."

He glanced down at her. His sage green eyes looked almost silver as he studied her face with an intensity that sent shivers of awareness through her. She'd swear this man could read her very soul. "You haven't asked me anything about Tim—"

Jack raised his hand. "If you're talking about that kiss— I… You…" His Adam's apple bobbed as if he had something stuck in his throat. Then anger sparked in his eyes and his voice rose an octave. "Why the hell hasn't that…that…fiancé of yours—"

"Yesterday I told Tim I couldn't marry him. I ended our engagement."

Jack stopped as if he'd rammed into an invisible barrier. In three seconds his expression ran the gamut from surprise to joy to uncertainty. His eyebrows dipped low. "Why? Because of Nightmare Man?"

Because I'm falling in love with you. But she couldn't tell Jack that. If he didn't feel the same, it would break her heart, and right now her emotional strength was shaky enough without adding that burden. "I can't promise him a future—I'm not certain I have one."

"You'll have one," Jack declared with such conviction she almost believed it was a fact instead of only a possibility. Her spirits lifted. Jack had a way of restoring her hope whenever it seemed she'd depleted the last of it.

She loved him for that. "I'm not certain what my future holds, but I am sure of one thing. I'm not the woman I was before I came to Alder Gulch. My innocence, my naiveté are gone…forever. I'm not the woman Tim fell in love with, not the woman he wanted for his wife."

Then he's the world's biggest fool, Jack thought. But what about Andrea's feelings for Tim Freyton? Were they different? Or had everything she'd learned about herself these past few days overwhelmed her to the point where she was incapable of deciphering one feeling from the next? That kind of shock would throw anybody off kilter.

Jack started walking again. Andy fell into step beside him, and having her there felt so natural, so satisfying, he knew he'd always want her there. But fear gripped his heart. What if he pressed his feelings for her?

He recalled with blood-stirring vividness the way she'd kissed him a short while ago. He recognized genuine passion when he held it in his arms, but did her desire arise from affection for Jack Starett, Jr., the man, or was it the result of the incredible bond they shared? He stared at the toes of his snakeskin boots, kicking up dust with every step. He couldn't discount the risk factor; danger was a potent aphrodisiac. Anyone might be swept away on its unpredictable tide.

But once her world was on course again, would Andy realize she still loved Freyton? He shoved his hand through his hair.

Like a giant spotlight, the sun hung over Alder Gulch, accentuating the eerie quietude on Main Street, and reminding

Jack he had more than Andy's rebounding heart to worry about. Her very life was at stake. Before they could even confront the issue of a future together, they had to lay the past to rest. They had to beat Nightmare Man.

Minutes later they were inside the Golden Broom's dining room. It was as deserted as the town, and without all the usual clamor of people, Andy realized a lot of money had been spent to make this restaurant and bar look rustic and old.

"At last, some customers." Red stood behind the counter, rummaging in the cash register. He slammed the till drawer shut and squinted at them. "Hotel's standing empty—had to cancel a whole day's reservations. This murder business is destroying my profit schedule."

"Speaking of the murder." Jack bent over, planting his palms on the counter. "Did you know someone stole the bullet that killed Coop?"

"Someone…?" Caught totally off-guard, Red stiffened, his mustache twitched and he leaned away from Jack. "This is the first I've heard of that. You think Duke or Gene stole it when you left them alone—while I was calling the sheriff?"

If this was the first Red had heard of the stolen bullet, then why, Jack wondered, did he have such a ready answer to his own whereabouts? "I'm not accusing anyone."

Red frowned. "Then just what are you doing?"

Jack straightened, retreating a step away from the counter. "Just asking if you knew anything about it."

"Well, I don't." Red smiled uneasily, glancing toward Andy. "I won't be happy until this whole mess is laid to rest. Man can't make a living anymore—what with murderers running around killing his friends."

"Red Yager, ya heartless cuss. All yer thinkin' about is yer profits, and poor Virgil Cooper ain't even buried yet," Minna Kroft reprimanded as she marched through the swinging bar doors and over to join them. "You ain't the only one with canceled reservations. So jest quit yer grousing. Sheriff Birdsill assures me he'll be allowin' tourists back into town in another day or so.''

"Two days or more?" Red groaned. "Meanwhile, I've got maids standing around twiddling their thumbs and I'm paying top dollar for my chef to waste time making sandwiches for Birdsill and his deputies like this restaurant was a blasted deli.''

Red rolled his neck and drew a long breath, releasing it slowly a moment later. His expression lightened and he put on his usual jovial manner, a deportment, it struck Andy, that was a practiced act.

Grinning, he grabbed hold of three menus. "Least I can do is see that my real customers get proper service. You've got your pick of the house today, folks. Which table will it be?''

Jack cleared his throat and looked sheepish. "None for Ms. Hart or me.''

"Oh?" Red's mustache seemed to sag. "Then what can I get the two of you?''

Andy grimaced. "Some sandwiches…to go.''

The ruddiness of Red's cheeks darkened to a deep magenta.

"We're going into the foothills for a picnic," Andy blurted out as though it were somehow her fault that the restaurant had no customers. What was she doing? She didn't owe these people an explanation.

"The foothills?" Red considered her with a squinted gaze that went beyond curious.

But Minna glanced from Andy to Jack with the look of someone who discerned romance in the air. Inexplicably, Andy felt a need to deny this. "Jack's taking me horseback riding. I haven't had much chance since I was a teenager.''

Minna smiled as smugly as a fat cat. "I see.''

Red also had a knowing look in his eyes, but Andy couldn't detect the source of it. He opened a menu and pointed to the listing of sandwiches, then instead of asking what they wanted to order, he said, "Wouldn't be riding out to the old Wood-worth place, would you?"

Andy's breath caught, but Jack found his voice right away, and somehow he managed to keep it level. "Why do you ask?"

Red shrugged, squinting again. "Rumor's going around town that Ms. Hart is actually Arlo and Marcy Woodworth's little girl. Any truth to that?"

Andy felt heat shoot into her face as she jerked her head toward Jack. He'd narrowed his eyes, but she could almost hear the cogs whirling through his mind; they were likely spinning as fast as her own.

Should she deny the rumor? No. What was the point of continuing to keep her identity a secret? The note left in her room invalidated any safety that might have existed in the element of surprise. In fact, now it was probably wiser to let everyone know who she was. There might be one or more people who'd actually look out for her welfare. "The rumor is correct. I am Leandra Woodworth."

"Well, hang me for a polecat." Red slapped the counter. "If this hasn't been some kind of week."

"No. It can't be true." Mouth agape, Minna stared at Andy, then shook her head. "You ain't Marcy's daughter. Little Lee Lee had them same crazy-colored eyes as Arlo. Yer eyes are both blue."

"Tinted contacts," Andy explained.

Minna's hand went to her chest as she digested the news, still shaking her head, getting used to the idea. "Where you been all this time? What you been doin'? How's Eloise?"

Andy sighed at the mention of her grandmother. "Gram died two months ago. Her heart."

Minna made a sad face. "Well, now, I'm right sorry to hear that. I was fond of Eloise. Yep, that's a real shame. I always wondered what become of you two. Imagine, Marcy's little girl writin' historical romance novels."

"Yeah," Red added. "Imagine."

He seemed as stunned as Minna, but, Andy reminded herself, the man was a good actor. "It sounds like you both knew my parents well."

Red laid an order pad on the counter. "Everybody in this town knows everybody else well."

"Ain't that the truth." Minna snorted. "The rumor mill in this town is better than any old newspaper."

"But my mother didn't grow up in Alder Gulch." Andy remembered. "Daddy met her in Missoula."

"At college," Minna mused. "My, but she was a pretty little thing. Real head turner. Your daddy was the envy of near every young buck in town."

Andy gazed pointedly at Red. Had he been one of the young bucks who'd envied her father? Who'd pressed his interest in her mother to the point of murder?

Red blushed, but quickly recovered, squinting hard at Andy as if something had just occurred to him. "So that's why you wanted to see some photographs of the town twenty years back. You're here looking into the murders. Got a new lead or something?"

"You mean she remembers who Nightmare Man is?" Minna asked eagerly.

"No. Nothing like that." Andy raised her hands in protest. "I only learned who I was after I arrived in town."

Red sniffed, glanced at Jack, then back at Andy. "Then you're not riding out to inspect the old homestead? As Arlo's only heir, I'd imagine it still belongs to you."

Minna frowned at Red, who didn't seem to notice.

With all that had been happening, Andy hadn't even thought about that, but she highly doubted the ranch still belonged to her. There was no way Gram would have continued paying the property taxes.

Would you, Gram? Not when you had no intention of ever returning to Montana. Not when you'd done your best to per-

suade me never to set foot inside this state. Not when you were trying to keep our whereabouts secret. She could hear Gram say, *Know when to cut your losses, girl. Sometimes the prize isn't worth the price tag.*

Who did own the Flying W now?

"Actually, since you've suggested it, Red..." Jack stepped up to Andy and gazed down at her. "Would you like to see what's left of your childhood home?"

Her heart hitched at his words, but she took his lead. "Yes, I think I would. I'm sure one of these two can tell us how to get there."

AN HOUR AND A HALF LATER, food packed in their saddlebags, Jack was astride his Appaloosa and Andy a roan mare. Red's directions had them traveling east out of town toward the Madison Mountain Range in the distance. The day had gotten away from them, and they were getting a much later start than Jack had wanted. It would probably be dusk before they headed back.

As the horses cantered side by side along the road, Andy bounced awkwardly like a first-time rider. Several minutes passed before she began relaxing and riding with her old finesse. Heat pressed her back, but she felt cold inside. Anxious. The steady clomp of the horses' hooves on the hard-packed road and the occasional squeak of the leather saddle seemed only to add to her dread.

"You handled yourself well when Red dropped his bombshell." Jack's compliment intruded on her anxiety, scattering it. "But you seem a little tense now."

"I'm okay. Did you notice the odd look Minna gave Red when he said I still might own the Flying W? What do you suppose that was about?"

"No idea." Jack shrugged. "But it was curious."

"What do you think of Red?" While she had fielded Red's

questions, Jack had quietly stood to one side, observing. "Is he Nightmare Man? Or just the relater of town gossip?"

Jack lifted his Stetson a notch higher on his forehead. "I'm not sure. He was quick with an alibi for the missing bullet, but he seemed genuinely surprised about your being Leandra Woodworth."

"But was he surprised? He's a pro when it comes to hiding his feelings."

"Yeah, I wouldn't want to play poker with him." The old frustration skittered through Jack. What they needed was some proof. If only Andy could remember. He realized she was probably thinking the same thing. Her knuckles were white on the reins. He wished he could ease her tension, get her mind on something else.

He drew an unsteady breath, smelling the familiar scents of horses and leather and dust. He loved Montana fervently— every stick, every rock, every creek, every rolling hill and vast mountain. He was starting to love this woman with the same kind of passion.

The inside of his mouth felt wet and his blood beat hot at every pulse point. He longed to loosen the ribbon that bound her glorious hair at the nape of her neck, to kiss her in just that spot.

"This must be the juncture Red mentioned." Andy cut through his thoughts.

Jack calculated they'd ridden a quarter mile out of town. He assured her she was right and they turned southward. "Come on, I'll race you."

Accepting the challenge, Andy pressed her horse to a gallop and soon they were fairly flying over the rolling hillsides that meandered into the distance like huge swelling waves of green and umber. Near the foothills were clumps of alders. And their destination.

They were laughing by the time they'd reached the last knoll. Jack reined in, easing the horse to a canter. Andy did the same. Her gaze went automatically to the clump of alders, but something else caught her attention. "Jack, look. Just cresting the knoll. Riders."

Jack followed her pointing finger with his gaze. "I'd say the lanky one is Duke Plummer. So the other must be Gene Mott."

"What are they doing out by my parents' old homestead? Do you suppose one of them bought the place by paying the land taxes?"

"I can't imagine it was worth much, but I wouldn't put anything past these two. Why don't we have a little chat with them?"

Jack veered into the path of the other two riders, who reined to a stop as he and Andy approached. She plastered a smile on her face, but the sight of the rifle each man carried in their saddle holsters sent a bead of sweat trickling down her spine.

Gene Mott sat the saddle with the ease of a man who had full use of both his legs. He wore a huge white hat, likely to protect his fair skin from the unrelenting sun, but the hat and his long-sleeved shirt were sweat stained and streaked with dust, as if he'd been toiling at some physical labor, not merely riding a horse on a warm summer day. Duke, also, had a sweat-dirtied shirt and dark smudges on his forehead and nose.

"Out to enjoy our glorious country, I see." Gene tipped his hat. "How is that book coming?"

"It's coming," Andy answered in a guarded voice.

"Perhaps I could help it along." Gene's smile didn't reach his eerily pale eyes. "I recall you expressed an interest in my Alder Gulch diaries. If you'd care to come by the house tomorrow and take a look at them...?"

Andy tensed at the implied threat in the invitation, her stomach dropping to her toes, but somehow she managed to keep her expression pleasant. Was Gene Mott just a strange man, given to quirks of personality—insufferably rude one moment and overtly friendly the next? Or was he Nightmare Man—playing some sick, psychotic game with her?

Either way, Andy was interested. "I'd like that very much."

"Good. Around two, then?"

"We'll be there," Jack answered for her. Ignoring Andy's bemused expression and Gene's darkening one, he leaned forward on the saddle horn. He didn't care if the whole town thought him rude, he'd be damned if he'd let Andy spend any time anywhere alone with either of these men. Now that she'd admitted to her true identity—whether or not she liked it—*he* was her brand-new shadow. "I was kind of hoping we'd run into the two of you."

Duke and Gene exchanged an uneasy glance as if they'd been caught doing something nefarious. This was the second time Jack had had that impression about these two men.

Duke toyed with his reins. "Why is that?"

Andy pushed her hat to the back of her head and directed her attention to Duke. "Jack and I visited your house this morning. We wanted to ask you something about…scorpions. You see, someone put one in my bed the other night."

Gene drew a sharp breath.

Duke jerked his gaze to Andy. "Jeez, who'd pull a nasty trick like that on a pretty young thing like you?"

"I don't know. We thought if we could find where the scorpion came from…"

"Don't look at me." Duke's rugged face was all innocence.

"Of course not. It's just that Red said you gave him the scorpion in his bar."

Warily, Duke pulled his hat from his head and wiped his brow with the sleeve of his dirty shirt. "That I did."

"He said it was one of four you brought back from an excursion down south. He says you gave one to someone else and kept two for yourself."

Plummer shook his head. "Red's mistaken. I brought only

two scorpions home from Florida. I gave him the healthy one. The other died. I mounted it.''

The one they'd seen on the shelf in his garage. Andy shivered.

''Are you sure?'' Jack asked, his Appaloosa prancing in a circle.

Duke plopped his brown hat back onto his head. ''Of course I'm sure.''

''Something eating at you today, Jack?'' Gene asked. ''You sound downright hostile.''

Jack shifted his gaze from the rifle near Gene's leg, then up to his face. ''The bullet that killed Coop has been stolen.''

Gene's icy blue eyes widened. ''What do you mean—stolen? From the sheriff?''

''No.'' Jack glanced at Duke. ''Before the sheriff arrived.''

''Before—'' Gene's hands relaxed on his reins and he smiled coldly. ''Oh, I see. You think one of us took it.''

A nasty, nervous chuckle spurted out of Duke. Then he scowled at Jack. ''Prove it.''

''I don't have to prove it.'' Jack's voice was frosty. ''But the sheriff knows I left the three of you in charge of the murder scene. He'll figure it out.''

''There's nothing to figure out.'' Gene spoke calmly. ''None of us had any reason to kill Virgil Cooper. He was a longtime friend.''

''That's right,'' Duke echoed, tugging his hat lower on his forehead. ''Hell, how do we know you didn't shoot Coop and steal the bullet yourself?''

''You don't.'' Jack's smile was forced and unfriendly.

''Then I guess we've reached an impasse, gentlemen.'' Gene shrugged and took a solid grip on his reins. ''Ms. Hart, see you tomorrow.''

When they'd ridden out of earshot, Jack said, ''Did you notice how sweaty and dirty those two were?''

''Like they'd been toiling at some physical labor. I thought

Gene was paraplegic. Am I wrong? Does he actually have the use of his legs?"

"Not to my understanding." Jack pulled his Stetson lower on his head. "And what about the scorpions? Who's lying? Red or Plummer?"

"I don't know. Remember Red and Minna saying everybody in this town knows everyone else's business. Do you think the whole town knows who murdered my parents? That they've banded together from some sort of misplaced civic loyalty and are keeping it secret?"

Chapter Eleven

Jack sat back on his saddle and gazed down at Andy with tender eyes. "The whole town covering up? I doubt it. First of all, that would make every citizen in Alder Gulch an accessory to murder. Secondly, it assumes they all thumbed their noses at the law, at your grandmother and your father—native daughter and son of the very town you'd have me believe they were protecting. Is that really logical, sweetheart?"

"Oh, I suppose I'm grasping at straws." Her gaze drifted over the alder grove cradled against the foothills, across the bleak remains of her childhood home that from this distance looked like half a dozen other burned-out homesteads she'd seen as she'd driven through the Western states in the past two months. "But I can't help thinking someone must know something."

"Someone did." Jack lifted his reins and clicked his tongue. The Appaloosa started forward.

Did? Past tense? Despite the heat of the sun, a chill rushed over Andy as she hollered after Jack, "Virgil Cooper?"

He glanced over his shoulder and nodded. "It seems more and more possible."

She would like to think he was right, that the bullet that had killed the photographer had never been meant for her. She urged the mare to action and caught up with Jack. "What about Minna Kroft? She said she was fond of Gram. Maybe she could tell us some of the gossip going on around the time just before my parents were killed.''

"We'll have a talk with her when we get back to the motel.''

They descended the hillside, leveling out on a road that must once have been regularly traveled, but had over the years been slowly reclaimed by Mother Nature. On the left side of the road barbed wire clung to a row of rotted posts that stumbled along the dry ditch like drunken miners, leading to an equally dilapidated welcome arch made of peeled lodgepole pines.

The Flying W Ranch.

Butterflies collided in Andy's stomach and she strove for something to occupy her mind, something other than the fear that was rearing through her with every step the mare took toward the welcome arch. Jack was gazing at the ground. "What are you looking at?''

"Mott and Plummer were definitely here. There are two clear sets of fresh horses' hooves in the dirt. Coming and going.''

The sudden, odd feeling that someone was watching them raised the fine hair on Andy's neck. Reflexively, she glanced over her shoulder at the hill above. If someone was there, she couldn't see them. Her nerves playing tricks? She applied her attention back to Jack. "Why were they both carrying rifles?''

Jack could tell she was rattled, and he didn't want to frighten her any further, but she had to know the dangers in this country. He patted his own rifle. "We're pretty far from town. Could be grizzlies, or wolverines, or rattlers out here.''

"Being prudent, then. Like us." Perhaps…but it didn't explain how either man had gotten so dirty. A trickle of sweat traveled between her breasts. The heat of the day and fast riding? That might explain some of the sweat on Gene and Duke, but not all of it. Jack was right. Their suspects had looked like laborers on a prison chain gang.

They rode beneath the welcome arch and started down the driveway. "Jack, if someone has purchased this property, why leave it in ruins with the Flying W sign still hanging—if somewhat precariously—from the arch?"

"That's what I've been wondering. According to what Wally and I could dig up, your great-grandfather won this plot of land in a poker game. It's said to have an abandoned mine on it, but that the mine was played out long before that infamous card game."

A memory flashed into Andy's mind and she craned her neck toward the clump of alders. There it was: the faint trickling of water. She smiled at Jack. "Daddy used to pan for gold in that creek out back. He wore a hunk of gold on a chain around his neck and told his friends that he'd panned it right here on his own property."

Interest spread across Jack's face. "Had he?"

Andy considered, trying to recall, then shrugged. "I was five years old. I really don't know."

Her attention winged to the rubble pile that had been her childhood home. The river-rock fireplace still stood, looking the worse for wear. Rocks had fallen from its face, leaving its misshapen chimney lifting toward the vast blue sky like an outstretched hand seeking help from the heavens.

Her hands dampened on the reins. Bits and pieces of memory, long-forgotten images of how the house had once looked, flicked through her mind like a handful of double-exposed Polaroid pictures, and Andy wanted to turn the horse around and ride hell-bent for town.

But a voice inside her head stopped her, a voice that sounded like Gram's. *This house can't hurt you now, Andy. But it might give you the knowledge you need to bring your parents' murderer to justice.*

Armed with fresh resolve and the strange, certain knowledge that Gram was watching protectively over her, Andy climbed down off the horse. Jack did the same. He grabbed his saddlebag and flung it across his shoulder, then strode toward Andy's mare.

Andy glanced across the rubble pile inside the foundation. It was littered with mysterious, deformed objects, all blackened and rotting, some of whose identity she guessed by remembering the positions of the rooms in conjuncture with the fireplace—bedsprings near the front porch, the stove and refrigerator near the back.

Surprisingly, the fire hadn't completely destroyed all the timbers, but she knew the wood would be rotted and she stepped with care over the singed foundation, then moved gingerly through the rubble. Her boots sank in the soft debris, one toe thudding into something solid. She leaned over, spotted a cast-iron kettle and lifted it by the swinging handle.

Didn't you make tea in this, Gram? Andy hooked the kettle over her left arm as a sense of loss swept through her, weakening her knees. She ought to be desensitized by time and distance, but she doubted she ever would be. It wasn't the material things she'd lost in this fire, but her childhood. Her parents. Tears sprang into her eyes and she moved blindly across the uneven rubble, the kettle bumping against her hip.

Out of nowhere, panic awoke. It started in the pit of her stomach and inched upward, spiraling outward and prickling her skin. And with it came something equally frightening: the very memories she'd come here seeking. She was five again, stumbling from her bed, seeing, hearing. Hearing. She covered her ears to block out the sounds of that horrible night twenty years ago, sounds now blaring inside her head like a stereo she couldn't shut off. The cast-iron kettle slipped down to her elbow.

"No, no, no, no," she murmured, staggering toward the foundation edge near the area that had once been the kitchen. Without warning the solid footing beneath her left foot disappeared as if she'd stepped over the edge of an unseen abyss, stepped into nothingness. She squealed and leapt back.

Rubble dropped with a clatter, raising dust and a foul rotting odor and robbing Andy of the memories she'd been reliving. Relief and frustration wrestled for control of her emotions as she gaped at the newly formed hole and knew she was staring into what had once been the cellar stairwell.

"What the hell—?" Jack hurried over to her. "Are you okay?"

"I—" But Andy broke off, her heart jumping into her throat.

As the last of the falling debris settled, there came from the cellar floor the unmistakable rattle of a diamondback. Then another and another.

"Holy—" She hightailed it out of the foundation, relishing the feel of solid ground. She stomped her feet, dislodging some of the debris from her boots, but her gaze remained on the hole. "I'm fine. That's our old root cellar. It's more of a cave dug into the dirt. Gram once told me an occasional rattlesnake or rabid prairie dog would burrow through. Looks like the snakes have taken it over now."

"Well, they aren't likely to bother us as long as we don't bother them. I'll tether the horses, then we can eat."

Andy doubted she could eat a thing, but she nodded. The snakes stirred again and she took another step back from the foundation. The proximity of the vipers was daunting, and the thought she'd been so close to recalling who Nightmare Man was and had lost it was infuriating and frustrating. And yet, that strange, comforting sense that Gram was with her persisted, consoling and soothing her. She took another step back.

Jack had just reached the horses when he heard the crack of a rifle shot, immediately followed by a metallic thunk. He jerked around. "Get down!"

But Andy was already falling, straight backward, her left arm outflung, the kettle flying off her fingertips, her right hand clutching her chest.

Terror tightened Jack's scalp. "Andy!"

"GOODBYE, LEE LEE." Nightmare Man grinned as he watched the woman hit the ground. Stretched on his stomach on the knoll above the Flying W ranch, not even feeling the rocks digging into his stomach and thighs, he shifted the rifle against his shoulder until he could see the man in its high-powered scope.

"Your turn, junior." He zeroed in on the man's broad chest. It was easier to hit a still target, but he supposed it was natural for the man to be rushing to the fallen woman.

With sweet anticipation he pulled the trigger. The jolt of recoil bit into his shoulder, but as he watched he laughed. Dead on. Jack's body jerked. His step hitched and he fell like a dropped rock, landing on Andy.

Just one more thing. The smell of his sweat stung his nostrils. He aimed the rifle at the two skittish horses and fired at the ground near their hooves. The mare whinnied, then bolted down the driveway; as she hit the old road to town, the Appaloosa was gaining on her.

Chapter Twelve

Amid the dust settling in Jack's nostrils he detected an odd, flowery sweet fragrance like...perfume? And it wasn't Andy's. Dear God, Andy! He had her pinned to the ground, his body covering hers in the classic position for making love. What he felt at the moment was anything but loving. Fear was tearing through his heart, ripping out his guts.

His first impulse was to roll off her and attend her wound, pull her to safety. But that was the problem. They were out in the open. The only cover—the alder grove—was at least sixty yards away. Whoever had shot them had done so with deadly intent and was likely watching, probably through a high-powered rifle scope, to see if he'd accomplished his feat.

"Andy," he whispered near her ear.

Beneath him, Andy moaned. He felt it more than heard it. He eased his weight onto his forearms and lifted his chest from hers, the movement slow, hopefully indiscernible from a distance. He was rewarded with a gasp from her. "Where were you hit?"

"Hit?" She sounded confused.

"Shot," he clarified hoarsely, holding his breath, praying against the odds that her wound was minor.

Shot? Is that what had knocked her off her feet as if she'd stepped on a banana peel? Something had definitely struck her in the chest. A bullet? With an effort, she inhaled. Wasn't that odd? There was the hint of flowery sweet perfume—Gram's White Shoulders—in the air. "Am I bleeding?"

A furious curse tore through Jack's mind. Was her life seeping out of her? He needed to know. To stop it. He dare not find out. Not yet. But soon. Soon. "Don't move, sweetheart. We need to play dead for a few minutes…and hope he doesn't come down to finish the job."

What little breath she'd managed to tug in beneath Jack's weight and the pain in her chest evaporated in a wave of fresh terror. "Can't you get your rifle?"

"The horses were run off."

Panic exploded inside Andy. She could not, would not, lie here like a wounded deer waiting to be finished off. She shoved at Jack and gained just enough space to scramble out from under him. As if she were five years old again, she knew the only thing that would save her was to run and hide.

Seeking shelter, she fled for the alder grove. Jack wasted no time following, covering her every movement, shielding her body with his larger one. There were no sharp cracks of rifle fire at his back. Andy darted through the trees and came to a stop at the creek. Breathless, she bent over gasping.

Jack grasped her by the shoulders and spun her around. The terror on his face fled, replaced by confusion. Her shirt and jeans were greasy and grimy, but not bloody. There was no blood on her anywhere. He tossed his head back, let out a groan of relief and dragged her into his arms. "Thank you, God."

Andy snaked her arms around his middle, clinging to him.

"When I saw you go down…" Jack pulled back and gazed at her. "How…?"

Andy thought again about the scent of White Shoulders she'd noticed. Gram? But that couldn't account for the bullet not striking her, or for the bruising ache on her breastbone. *Of course.* "The kettle. I'll bet it has a real nice dent in it."

Jack remembered the metallic thunk. "It saved your life."

"That and my guardian angel." *Gram.*

Jack's eyes softened. "An angel, huh?"

"Don't you believe in angels?"

"Never thought about it." Jack thought about it now, recalling the unfamiliar perfume he'd smelled. There was no explaining that, nor the fact that he—usually as surefooted as they came—had hooked the toe of his boot on something buried in the dirt and tripped.

Andy was trembling. The horror of being shot at was sinking in, the shock deepening. Jack pulled her closer, then froze at the sound of a galloping horse approaching. They had to take cover. Now. Across the creek a cluster of large boulders presented the perfect spot. Holding her in the crook of his arm, he hurried Andy along, splashing through the shallow creek and up the slight rise.

What was that behind the boulders—a cave? Hope bounced inside Jack. But seeing that three sides of the opening were supported by railroad ties, he knew it was not a cave.

"Daddy's mine," Andy confirmed.

They scrambled inside, the cooler air immediately grazing Andy's overheated face. She felt weak with terror; her heart was in her throat, her lungs heaving. "Jack, we're trapped. This is a dead end."

"Just keep going." He urged her deeper into the shaft. "He won't risk coming in here if he can't see us." The toe of his boot bumped metal. The object clinked, then knocked against his shin.

Andy jumped. "What was that?"

Wincing, Jack scanned the ground, but it took several seconds before his eyes adjusted to the darkness and he spied the object he'd struck. "A pickax."

He warned himself against getting excited about the possible weapon. It was likely old and rotted and rusted. He grasped the tool, and surprise zipped through him. "This handle is as sturdy and smooth as a seasoned baseball bat."

He lifted it toward the light spilling across the mouth of the mine. "It might even be new."

Andy was a dark shadow behind him. "Is someone working this mine?"

Jack had no time to answer. Ripping through the quiet from somewhere near the burned-out house came a shout of rage as bone-chillingly inhuman as the cry of a wounded animal.

Jack's body tensed, his fingers white-fisting the ax handle. Nightmare Man had just discovered they weren't dead. Supposing he knew about the mine shaft and guessed their hiding place? Came after them? No. He was too smart to risk one or the other of them getting away and being able to accuse him.

Being able to accuse him. For fifteen years that need had ruled Jack's life. *He* was so close. Just through the creek, through the alders. *If I belly-crawled to the grove. I could see his face. Know my father's murderer.* Reflexively, Jack started toward the adit.

Alarmed, Andy caught his arm. "Where are you going?"

As though her touch had brought him out of a trance, Jack shook himself and gazed down at her. What was he doing?

"I know you want to charge out there and fell him with one blow, but a pickax is no match for bullets."

"God, I…" The mindless fury roiling through Jack unnerved him; giving it free rein was tantamount to disaster. Maybe death. And he'd thought Andy was the only one suffering from shock. He drew several deep breaths. Their only chance of surviving was outwitting the man, and until he calmed down they didn't have that chance.

Jack jerked off his Stetson, flung it behind them into the mine and gazed down at her as he ran his fingers through his thick hair. "Get back into the shadows. I'm going out to the boulders to see if he's coming this way."

Andy's pulse leapt. She'd rather he stayed here with her, but if Nightmare Man was coming, they'd need another plan. "Keep low."

"Count on it." Grasping the pickax like a club, Jack hunched down and moved to the adit, stopping just inside the shaft and studying the terrain outside before stealing to the boulders. Shafts of setting sunlight poked his eyes as he flattened himself against the warm rocks.

Straining to hear anything above the trickling of the creek, he detected a soft metallic clank somewhere near the house. He breathed more easily. Feeling relatively safe, Jack risked a look between two of the boulders. He had a perfect view of the fields and mountain range in the distance, but the alder grove effectively blocked the area he wanted to see.

Frustration threatened again. Inaction went against his grain, his very nature; he hadn't earned a Pulitzer for being passive. But what could he do?

The shout came so unexpectedly, Jack jolted and dropped to his knees.

"I know you're out there somewhere." Nightmare Man's voice was an unidentifiable scream resounding from the area around the house. "This isn't finished!"

Seconds later the sound of a horse trotting into the distance pulled Jack to his feet. He peered again through the gap between the boulders, but all he could make out was a cloud of dust disappearing down the road.

"What's happening?" Andy's voice echoed inside the shaft, louder than she'd meant. Although heat had seeped out of the air with the sun's descent, sweat trickled down her neck and she yanked off her hat and tossed it down beside Jack's.

"He's leaving." Jack strode toward her. Most of the women he knew would be hysterical by now, but though she had to be terrified, there was nothing in Andy's expression that showed she was ready to throw in the towel.

She stepped toward him. "Really leaving, or circling back?"

Jack set the pickax aside and drew his arms around her. "If he's smart—and we both know he is—it's damned certain he hightailed it back to town. He needs to resume some pretense of normality—he won't risk our discovering tomorrow that he'd been missing during the crucial hours.''

The knot in Andy's stomach lessened.

Jack nuzzled her soft hair with his chin. Even with grit and grime from the burned-out house clinging to her clothes, there was a delicate clean scent about Andy, and one whiff stirred his blood.

"It's nearly night," she murmured, her voice laced with hope. "Shouldn't we start walking back to town?"

Jack hated to burst her bubble, but they'd talked about this before. "It's too far of a walk to risk in the dark without a gun. Predators."

Andy shivered against him and buried her face in his shirt. She'd known he was going to say that. Give her good old western Washington anytime, where the only predators she'd had to elude at night were human. She leaned back and stared up at him. "Where will we spend the night?"

"Here—unless you have a better suggestion."

She could think of none. "At least you'll be with me."

He dipped his head and captured her mouth in a long, full kiss that left his voice raspy. "Every second."

Andy smiled at him.

Jack realized she was getting harder to see. Dusk was descending fast. "Before it's totally dark, I want to go and look at his horse's tracks. Maybe there will be some way to identify which horse he was riding and thus identify him."

"Then I'm coming, too."

Even in the dying light, Jack could see the determination he was growing to respect glinting in her eyes. He released her, grabbed the pickax and nodded. "But we have to be cautious."

Still trying to catch her breath from the kiss, Andy followed him to the adit. Her lips tingled and her blood felt heated for the first time in hours, but fear of what could await them outside the mine had her nerves taut.

Jack stopped and spun around, extending the pickax to her. "If it becomes necessary—just use this like you were swinging at a baseball."

"Let's hope he's as smart as you think and that it won't be necessary."

They left the shaft and descended the incline. Dusk had advanced, but a full moon was on the rise and she could see more than she would have thought possible. Her hands gripped the pickax handle and her pulse thundered in her ears, all but drowning out the quiet splashing of their feet as they crossed the creek. Ahead, Jack moved as stealthily as a stalking mountain lion.

Jack swept his gaze across the terrain, this way, then that. At the alder grove he crouched and peered through the trees. Andy did the same, whispering, "It looks deserted."

"Let's wait a few minutes and make certain."

Five minutes passed like five hours. Andy's knees were getting stiff from crouching when Jack murmured, "Stay here until I reach the foundation. I'll signal if it looks safe."

Her throat constricted, but she managed a nod.

Jack's large frame disappeared through the line of trees and emerged on the other side. He moved with measured pauses and at length arrived at the burned-out house. She watched him scan the area in all directions before he signaled her to come ahead.

In seconds she was beside him. Jack was hunkered down inspecting the ground. "Damn the sneaky bastard. He dumped our saddlebags and used them to obscure the horse's hoofprints."

In the light of the rising moon Andy could see the contents of their saddlebags scattered across the area. She went to see if anything was salvageable. Keeping her voice just above a whisper, she informed Jack, "We can forget about the sandwiches, and the wine bottle struck the foundation and shattered, but with the creek so near, we won't go thirsty and I've found a hunk of cheese and a package of crackers. And the skinny quilt Minna insisted we bring for our picnic.''

"Great. Ha." Jack's voice was also low, but sounded triumphant. "And I've found my canteen and my flashlight."

"Does the flashlight work?"

"I'll try it when we get back to the mine."

A coyote howled at the rising moon and Andy shivered. "Hadn't we better do that now?"

As they started back, Andy's foot struck something sticking up in the dirt. Moonlight glinted off its silvery surface. "Isn't this where you tripped?"

"Pretty much."

"Well, maybe this is the culprit." She bent and pulled free a half-looped piece of metal.

"What is it?"

"I can't tell." She jammed it into her pocket. Her gaze darted around. "Let's get out of here."

Jack took the pickax and the quilt and hurried her toward the alder grove. He stopped at the creek and filled the canteen, then seconds later they were back inside the mine. He laid the pickax aside, spread the thin blanket on the floor of the shaft, then tried the flashlight.

"It works." Andy blinked against the sudden brightness and grinned.

"All the comforts of home, ma'am," he said in his best Black Jack drawl. He sank to the quilt and patted the spot next to him.

Andy accepted his invitation. As she sat, the "something" she had jammed into her pocket jabbed her hipbone. She wriggled it free. Jack panned the light over the silver crescent-moon-shaped object. "A bracelet?"

Andy's attention was fully caught by the bracelet.

Jack joked. "You can't seriously think that little thing tripped a big galoot like me?"

She turned the bracelet in her hands, studying it, somehow recognizing it. She pointed to the inside of the band. "Shine the flashlight here."

"It's an inscription. To Eloise, Love Always, Ben." Andy's mouth went dry and her heart swelled. "Oh, Jack. This belonged to Gram. Grampa Ben gave it to her on their wedding day. I remember when I was a little girl that she always wore it, but I haven't seen it since the night of the fire. She must have lost it when she came to bring me home with her."

An inexplicable certainty struck Andy. Today Gram had saved not only her life, but Jack's. She clutched the bracelet to her heart. *Thank you, Gram.*

Seeing how much the bracelet meant to her, Jack reached for her left hand. "Then from this moment on, you should wear it."

The flashlight offered an ambience as soft as a candle's glow. Andy gazed into his eyes and her breath snagged. Without his asking for the bracelet, she handed it to Jack. He clasped it to her wrist. "It's too large."

"I inherited my lean bones from Mommy, my height from Daddy." Placing her right hand over Jack's, she squeezed the silver ends until the bracelet felt comfortably tight. "There."

"Beautiful." Jack turned her hand in his, then kissed her wrist above and below the bracelet. Delicious shivers sped up her arm and warmth spiraled into her heart. Somehow it seemed like a ceremony that would link them forever. She lifted her gaze to his and saw the longing. Its twin stirred inside her.

Jack cleared his throat, released her hand and grabbed the chunk of cheese from the quilt. He sliced off a wedge with his pocketknife and offered it to Andy. "Here, pretty lady."

"Pretty? Perhaps you'd like to borrow my contacts, Mr. Starett?"

"A little trail dust doesn't count." Jack took his clean handkerchief from his pocket, wet it with water from the canteen.

"A little trail dust?" Andy laughed, and brushed at her grimy clothing.

Jack caught her jaw with one of his big hands, and holding it gently, he wiped her forehead, her cheeks, her chin, lingering the cloth at her mouth, rubbing the tip of his thumb over her full lower lip. God, she took his breath away. He lowered his mouth to hers.

Andy's blood thrummed a sweet song through her veins, zipping tingles of pleasure to every part of her. Jack's big hands captured her face gently, possessively, and she melted into his kiss, opening her mouth, encouraging him to deepen the kiss, to taste her, to let her taste him.

Jack moaned and pulled away. "We'd better stop. I want you way too much to keep this up."

"I want you, too, Jack," Andy said breathlessly. "I want you to fulfill the promise of ecstasy that your kisses have hinted at from the very first. Please, Jack."

Jack groaned as if she'd wounded him. His breathing was ragged, and desire smoldered in his eyes, darkening them from silver-green to a color as lush and wild as the deepest forest. He reached for the ribbon at her nape and eased it down her back, releasing her hair, running his hands through the silken chocolate tresses. Then, drawing her against his chest, he kissed her neck where the ribbon had been.

Slowly his kisses circled her neck to her throat and he began unbuttoning her shirt. She wriggled out of her boots as Jack lavished kisses down her body, wet-hot touches inflaming every inch of her that was revealed with the shedding of her clothing.

Before now, she'd only written about the heady sensations

turning her insides to liquid fire, but for the first time in her life she was living her fantasies. In every way that she described her heroes giving her heroines pleasure, every stroke, every taste, every sensuous thrill, Jack was giving her now.

Jack dropped the last of her clothes beside the boots and disrobed as he stared at her breathtaking beauty. An ugly bruise was forming on her sternum, but her bare breasts shimmered white in the dim light, their tips rosy with invitation, pouty with need. His own need throbbed for release.

Andy's heart picked up its melodious thrumming as she stared at Jack's magnificent body that sported ebony hair in the most erotic places. He was a big man in every respect and the burning in her blood made Andy bold enough to rise onto her knees and play her fingertips over his muscled chest, his washboard stomach and lower, enjoying the sweet, hard feel of him, and eventually, the tangy taste of him.

Every pleasure that she described her heroines giving her heroes, with her mouth, with her tongue, with her touch, she bestowed on Jack—until on a velvety moan, he hauled her up the full length of his body, cupped her naked bottom with both his hands, lowered her to the quilt and moved between her open thighs.

Andy was unprepared for the thrill that swept her with their joining, unprepared for the need to have him deeper and deeper inside. She met his every thrust with equal eagerness, equal abandon, equal joy, until starbursts exploded inside her head and shot along every nerve ending, leaving her limp and happy.

Jack was slow to move off her. He wanted to prolong their oneness…into forever. This was a first. After making love with other women, he was always restless, eager to depart. Not now. Not with Andy. He kissed her temple.

She grinned up at him. "I didn't know it could be like this."

"Neither did I." Was this the way she would always be

with him? Or did their unique situation account for her abandon? Maybe it was the simple fact that she was on the rebound and needed reaffirmation of her desirability? Whatever it was, he didn't care to analyze. Not now. He felt himself growing hard inside her at the same time Andy twined her fingers behind his neck and pulled his mouth to hers.

Afterward, they dressed and ate all the cheese and crackers, sharing water from the canteen, touching and talking and laughing. Until Jack asked, "Have you remembered who he is?"

Andy's body went cold inside, all the warmth of their lovemaking gone in a wink, a question. Had his desire for her all been a part of his obsession? In the distance the coyote howled, sounding as forlorn as Andy suddenly felt. "No, Jack. I haven't remembered."

"It's all right. You will, sweetheart. We'd better get some sleep." Wrapped in the blanket, the pickax within easy reach, Jack snuggled his front to Andy's back and draped his arm over her waist. Although he soon heard her even breathing, his mind raced.

Who would have thought he'd fall in love with the daughter of the couple whose murder had precipitated his own father's death? What would his family say about it when he told them? Would they accept Andy for herself, love her as he did, or would they think his feelings for her were yet another phase of his obsession? The ultimate extension of his obsession?

The thought hit him like a slap across the brain. Was that how he really felt about Andy? Or was this his ego's way of protecting him if she decided it was Freyton she really loved?

Suddenly Andy stirred beneath his arm, rolled over onto her back. He knew she was awake. "Can't sleep, either?"

She rose up on one elbow. "Jack, what if *he* comes back tonight hoping to catch us sleeping?"

Chapter Thirteen

"I was just lying here thinking the same thing," Jack lied. He traced a fingertip along her jaw. Oh, the thought had crossed his mind, but it hadn't occupied it. Now he realized it should have—instead of ways to resolve an issue about Andy that would only be decided if and when Nightmare Man was permanently out of their lives. "I guess we'd better take turns keeping watch. I'll take the first shift."

"Only if you promise to wake me in a couple of hours."

Jack knew for certain he wouldn't be able to keep his eyes open much past that. Too few calories and an abundance of lovemaking had claimed most of his energy. He'd put both of their lives in jeopardy if he decided to let her sleep, then fell asleep himself. The image chilled him.

Right now his will to live, to more than survive, was stronger than usual. Andy's doing. "Considering the vigorous workout you put me through, sweetheart, I'd say a couple of hours will be about the limit before I'll need some shut-eye."

Jack's soft breath fanned her face and Andy sighed. Their lovemaking flashed into her mind, but she willed the images away. As sweet as the distraction had been, as tempting as Jack was, the idea of Nightmare Man coming upon them in that vulnerable state terrified her. "Two hours, then."

"Three." Jack relinquished the cover, stood and stretched. As Andy curled into the scant warmth of the quilt, he headed for the mine opening. The moon was high and full and offered a panoramic view of the surrounding terrain. He checked his watch and discovered, as he'd guessed, that it was nearly one. If Nightmare Man was coming it would be sometime before four in the morning.

After that the sky would start to lighten again.

Knowing Jack would be on guard, Andy felt her sense of calm returning. She rolled over onto her side again, snuggled into the quilt and was soon asleep.

Every now and then Jack glanced down at her. He didn't have to force himself to stay awake. The thought of Andy being taken from him was enough to do that.

As his gaze swept back across the fields for the hundredth time, he cursed the rippling of the creek. Under normal circumstances he would enjoy its relaxing babble, but now he found it an annoyance that interfered with his ability to hear as clearly as he'd like. The first hour stretched into the second and then into the third. Only once did his heartbeat kick into high gear—when a dark shape lumbered across a nearby field. He stood frozen for several seconds before identifying the grizzly.

As the third hour stretched toward the fourth, his eyelids grew heavy. Andy jerked up with a start at the touch of his hand on her shoulder. "He's here?"

"No sign of him, and if he was coming, he'd be here by now."

"What time is it?" Andy kicked off the quilt and stood.

"Around four."

She nodded, handed him the quilt, stretched, walked to the adit and peered out. The cool night air helped chase the residue of sleep from her eyes and her mind. The moon had disappeared over the mountains, but the sky was more charcoal than opaque.

Exhaustion claimed Jack within minutes.

At the sound of his even breathing, Andy felt a sudden

loneliness. She covered Gram's bracelet with her right hand. *How did I get to this point, Gram? Hiding in this mine as I once hid in the pantry—from the same awful man?* It was as if her life had gone full circle and led her back to the beginning. Or was it the end?

She glanced at the man lying mere feet from her—the one good thing in all this horror. The image of his lovemaking sprang into her head. But was tonight the only night they'd have together? Tears stung her eyes, and the dam she'd held back burst in a stream spilling down her cheeks. It wasn't Jack Nightmare Man wanted—any more than it had been Virgil Cooper he'd been after.

No one was more of a threat to him than she.

But why was she crying? Tears wouldn't help negate the hysterical amnesia that was keeping her from bringing the vile murderer to justice. She wiped her eyes with the backs of her hands and scanned the terrain beyond the boulders. Nothing stirred.

Anticipation kept her tense, and time seemed to move more slowly than the creek in August. The night grew colder. She rubbed her arms, then hugged herself in an attempt to sustain her body heat. She needed something useful to occupy her mind.

Andy closed her eyes, willing the memories to come, the ones that had surfaced while she'd stood in the burned-out shell of her childhood home. Damn. She could see that night so clearly, every awful detail...all except him. She was well enough acquainted with their suspects by now that if she could only see the outline of his body, a movement, a gesture, she'd probably be able to guess Nightmare Man's identity.

But he might have been a ghost, so elusively did he haunt her mind.

A moan from Jack jarred Andy, bringing her back to the moment, blinking. He didn't snore, but he had a tendency to mumble in his sleep. She stifled a grin and once more inspected the terrain for human predators.

An hour passed, then another. Her mind tended to drift to the feel of Jack's hands and mouth on her. Time and again she forced the distracting thoughts away. She had to stay alert, to protect this man she had fallen in love with as he had protected her.

Her back and leg muscles were growing stiff as the sun swept pale ribbons of light across the sky. She took one long, last glance out at the countryside, then turned around and gazed down at Jack.

His jaw was black with morning beard and his chest rose and fell in even intervals. His lashes were obscenely long for a man and, with his eyes closed, lay against his upper cheeks. He moaned again, and Andy could swear he'd said her name.

Suddenly aware that she probably looked a fright—hair unkempt, makeup smudged or gone—she found her red ribbon, finger-combed her hair and pulled it back as best she could without a mirror or brush, securing it at her nape as she had yesterday. Her eyes felt gritty. She popped out her contacts and folded them carefully in Jack's handkerchief.

"Jack, come on." She knelt beside him and gently jostled his shoulder. "It's daylight."

He opened his eyes and took in her face. "Morning, pretty lady."

"Morning, cowboy."

"I hope you got the license number of the truck that hit me." He struggled up, his body aching from tension, from glorious sex and from want of food, but Andy's bright smile gave him the energy to rise.

He folded the quilt, donned his Stetson and leaned over for the flashlight, accidentally flicking it on as he lifted it. The bright beam landed on a sidewall deep inside the shaft and showed a new cut in the rock. His eyebrows lifted at the discovery. "Someone *has* been working this mine."

Andy stood at the adit, gazing out. She spun at this remark. "What?"

He gestured for her to come to him. "See for yourself."

She followed Jack to the wall highlighted by the flashlight and stared in astonishment as he pointed out the areas where someone had been using the pickax. "Do you suppose this is what Gene and Duke were up to yesterday?"

"Anything's possible, but I don't see anything here to get excited about. 'Course, I'm no expert on precious metals."

Andy hugged herself. "Could we discuss this in the sunlight?"

"Sure, sure." Jack clicked off the flashlight and followed her outside, his mind drifting back to her question about Plummer and Mott. "I suppose it could explain the guilty looks on those two fellows every time I run into them."

Andy felt a flutter of excitement as strong as the ripple of the creek. They might finally—actually—be on to something important. "You think they've been conferring over this mine?"

"I don't know what to think." With Andy at his side, Jack splashed through the creek. Although the air was still cool, the day promised to be another scorcher. "I'm not convinced that Gene has the use of his legs. That kind of secret would be impossible to keep in a town the size of Alder Gulch. And if he is paralyzed from the waist down, how could he possibly get in and out of this mine—off and on his horse—without more assistance than Duke Plummer could offer?"

Andy's hope took a serious blow. "Who, then?"

"The answer to that might well lie in whose name is on the title to this piece of property." Jack kept a wary eye on the hillsides, looking in particular for any telltale flashes of light, like the reflection of the sun off a rifle barrel.

She, too, kept alert as they strode to the alder grove. "That should be pretty simple to check out."

"Yeah, there are several things we can check out today. But first we need to get back to town in one piece."

Her nerves tensed, but she made light of her fears. "Food and a bath—in that order—the minute we hit town."

"Me, too," Jack agreed.

They left the protection of the alder grove only after checking the surrounding hills and the general area nearby. Andy strode purposefully to the burned-out foundation. She found the kettle and lifted it, feeling more fortunate than ever—even with the tender bruise on her breastbone. "I think I'd like to keep this lucky charm."

As she turned to Jack, she caught sight of a dust trail coming toward them down the road, before she heard the motor of the car.

"Head for the trees," Jack said.

She dropped the kettle and ran. Breathless, they crouched behind the trees, peering out. Soon the car appeared, an all-terrain vehicle with the Madison County sheriff's office insignia on the doors.

Jack said, "It's Birdsill, or one of his deputies."

Relief swept Andy and she smiled and started to stand. Jack caught her by the hand. "Wait. Let them get out of the car before we show ourselves."

Minna Kroft's familiar mannish figure seemed to spring from the front passenger side of the car. "Yoo, hoo. Andy. Jack, ya out here?"

The driver's door and one of the back doors opened more slowly, the occupants less frantic in their movements.

"Birdsill," Andy said. "But who is that other man with him?"

At his first sight of the stocky man with the thick gray crew cut, Jack's grip on her went slack and he lurched to his full height, dragging her to her feet. "Wally Lester."

Andy felt as if a tremendous weight had been lifted from her chest.

They left the shelter of the trees, calling out as they showed themselves. Wally and Birdsill came on the run.

"Junior." Wally grasped Jack and grinned in relief. "Praise the Lord, you're all right. You are all right, aren't you?"

"Hungry, but otherwise A-okay." Jack clasped Wally on the shoulder. "What are you doing here?"

"Just wanted to see if you were making any progress." Wally gave him a look that said the truth could wait until they didn't have an audience. "When I arrived at your motel, Mrs. Kroft said you'd taken Ms. Woodworth for a picnic and she didn't expect you back anytime soon."

With this last Wally turned to Andy and extended his hand. "I've waited a long lot of years to lay eyes on you."

Andy wasn't certain if this was good or bad, but there was a warmth in Wally's brown eyes that reminded her of Gram's and she decided to give him the benefit of the doubt. She shook his hand. "Nice to meet you, too."

Wally grinned, but his expression wavered between relief and anxiety. "I have to tell you, when you didn't return—"

Minna cut him off. "I told Birdsill 'twasn't likely you'd've spent the night out here. Not with a perfectly good bed—" She broke off, her face flaming. "Well, now, I mean to say, something must've caused yer horses to run off back to the stable."

At this, Jack wheeled to Birdsill, who had been listening with a solemn expression in his yellow eyes. "If the horses came back to the stable, why didn't you send help last night?"

"No one told me about any of this until this morning."

Minna humphed. "And I didn't know till then, neither. I don't do bed checks on my lodgers, ya know."

"And I didn't know who to awaken in the middle of the night," Wally said in an apologetic tone.

The long hours of worry had taken their toll on Wally, and Jack, conscious of his old friend's high blood pressure, hated adding to his distress. But it was unavoidable. "Someone tried to kill us yesterday, Sheriff."

Minna gasped. Wally paled. Birdsill swore under his breath, and anger danced into his feral eyes, anger Jack would swear was directed at Andy and him. Curbing his own temper, Jack produced the kettle, pointed out the dent and related the story from the first gunshot to the last shouts of rage to their discovery of the obscured hoofprints.

Birdsill wrote it all down in his notepad, then lifted his head and scanned the hillside behind them. "He would have to have had a high-powered scope to draw a bead on you from there. And why risk it if he was such a poor shot?"

Minna shook her head, her fluffy hair flapping. "Don't make sense. A man smart enough to brush out his horse's prints wouldn't try shootin' two sittin' ducks—easy kills, ya might say—if he wasn't damned sure he'd hit his targets. Yet he missed ya both?"

Andy and Jack exchanged a glance. Jack thought about the shooting trophies on Minna's bookshelf, and his old suspicions of her not being what she seemed breathed new life. "It was dumb luck."

"Don't discount the will of God," Wally added.

Birdsill studied the kettle. "Neither of you saw the shooter?"

"No." Jack swallowed the frustration this question invariably brought. He heaved the cast-iron kettle and it sailed through the air, landing with a clank in the burned-out foundation, lifting a tiny cloud of sooty dust.

Birdsill frowned. "Did you at least recognize his voice?"

Andy heaved a disheartened sigh. "Not that, either."

The sheriff gave her a sympathetic smile. "I don't suppose you've remembered who he is?"

She shook her head, feeling the weight of her burden pressing down on her like an avalanche of snow.

"Well, now, that's too bad. Without something more concrete, we're still at square one." He put his notepad into his pocket and poked a finger at Jack, then Andy. "Coming out here was damned foolish. You're lucky it turned out as well as it did. So keep your noses out of this investigation."

"Really, Sheriff," Wally interjected.

Birdsill rounded on him. "I mean it, Mr. Lester. I've got no objection to a free press. But I won't tolerate amateurs doing my job."

Minna cleared her throat. "Let's get these two young people back to town, Sheriff. I'll bet they're hungry as baby birds."

"Yes." Andy gave Minna a grateful smile. "And I'd like a bath as soon as possible."

"Got hot coffee in a thermos." Minna hooked arms with Andy and started for the car.

"I mean what I say, gentlemen. Interfere one more time and I'll throw you all in jail." Birdsill tugged the bill of his hat down. "Now, let's go."

As soon as Jack, Andy and Wally were settled in the back seat, Jack gave Wally a look that told him anything he wanted to know would have to wait until the three of them were alone.

Two hours later, fed, showered, wearing clean clothes and running on caffeine, Jack and Andy sat at the table in his cabin. Wally refilled their coffee cups and retook his seat. "Now, Junior, what didn't you tell that sheriff?"

Jack rubbed his tired eyes and sighed. "I'm not sure it would interest him, but this morning we discovered someone has recently been working the mine."

Wally pulled on his nose. "And the significance of this is...?"

Jack shrugged, but Andy leaned forward on the table.

"Could the mine have been the motive behind the murder of my parents?"

Wally considered, then shook his head. "I doubt it. Twenty years have gone by. If the mine had been the motive, whatever was to be gained by it would have been taken long ago. No, the crime was too violent."

Frowning, Andy glanced at Jack. "I don't—"

Jack interrupted. "Violence denotes passion—a sudden eruption of emotion, like unleashed fury."

"Besides," Wally continued, "the mine wouldn't explain the murder of Karen Bradley—a young woman who looked strikingly like your mother."

Andy sat back, her fingers curling around her coffee mug. "Then maybe what Minna said about the young studs in town lusting after my mother is the right motive?"

"I believe it is. To my way of thinking, whoever did this took a shot with your mother and when she turned him down, maybe even laughed at him, he snapped."

"Daddy must have come in from the fields right after it happened." Andy swallowed over the lump in her throat.

Jack touched her arm, rubbing it comfortingly.

Wally raised an eyebrow at this. "Which of your suspects do you fancy, Junior?"

Jack made a noncommittal grunt. "Why don't you regale us with what you've found out about them? How about Duke Plummer?"

A manila envelope lay near Wally's elbow. He opened it and pulled out a sheaf of papers. "Let's see. He'd returned home after a four-year stint in the army just months before the Woodworths were married. His father had recently passed away from cancer. He moved in with his mother and took over her job of assistant at the museum, while mom took over her husband's job as curator. When she retired, the job passed to Duke."

"A mama's boy?" Jack asked.

Wally lifted his eyebrows. "No proof. He never married, but he has a married sister living in Virginia City."

"Can he handle a rifle?"

"He received the expert marksman badge while at Fort Bliss."

Jack took a swallow of coffee. "How about Red Yager?"

"By all accounts he's an upright citizen. He played the rodeo circuit throughout his teens and garnered several state rifle championships. Turned a penchant for rare guns into a profitable hobby. Inherited the hotel from his parents and remodeled it into what you see today."

"Ever married?"

"Not that I could find out. But rumor is he's fond of young blondes—like Karen Bradley."

"And we know either Duke or Red lied to us about the number of scorpions Duke brought into Alder Gulch." Jack sighed. He'd hoped Wally's information would allow them to eliminate someone from their list, but that hope was sinking fast. "Gene Mott?"

"The official story is that he fell off a horse and broke his spine, leaving him a paraplegic."

"The official story?" Andy frowned.

"Press releases," Jack explained. But something in Wally's voice stirred his interest. "Everyone I questioned about it when I first arrived here told me the same story. Are you saying it isn't true?"

"No. What I'm saying is that a few years back a couple of the tabloids ran stories about a drunk-driving incident. Mott sued both times and won both times."

Jack tapped the rim of his coffee cup. "I was hoping you were going to tell me the stories claimed the injury was faked."

"Well, that's the thing. The very fact that there's controversy over how he was injured makes me wonder how seriously he *was* injured. But hospital and doctor records are confidential and I can't lay my hands on any of them.''

Remembering Wally's illegal possession of the Bradley girl's police case records, he knew scruples weren't keeping Wally from laying his hands on the records. He just didn't know anyone who could get the information for him.

''So, we hit another wall.'' Andy rolled her neck. God, why couldn't she just see *his* face?

''Not necessarily, sweetheart. There are other ways to find out if Gene is faking or not.'' Jack glanced at Wally. ''What about Minna Kroft?''

''Minna?'' Andy reared back in surprise. ''Surely you don't suspect Minna of being Nightmare Man?''

Jack reached for his coffee cup and took a long swallow. *Why not Minna? She's the right age, and she stomped the scorpion to death before we could capture it and use it for evidence. And there are those rifle trophies.* While Andy knew all this, Jack realized she probably needed someone to trust, and Minna had been kind to her. He kept his voice gentle. ''Strictly to be on the safe side, I asked Wally to check her out.''

Andy scraped back her chair and stood. She walked to the sink and dumped out the rest of her coffee.

Wally referred to his notes. ''Minna moved here a year or so before your parents were killed. A widow. Her husband died in a car crash. Left her the money to buy this place. Apparently this was a favorite vacation spot of theirs.''

So much for how well Minna had known the Woodworths and Andy's grandmother. He'd like to scratch her off his suspect list, but how could he? He shoved back his chair and carried his own cup to the sink. ''About all we know is that all of our suspects had means and possible motive.''

Frustration filled Andy, pressing against her temples like some painful vise gripping tighter and tighter. She could solve this whole thing. *If* she could just remember. But she couldn't. "This is getting us no closer."

Jack caught her gently by the shoulders and spun her toward him. The disheartened flatness in her eyes tore at him. He knew some of her distress would leave when she'd had time to sleep. But right now she needed reassurance that they could figure out who Nightmare Man was before he figured out some way to stop them.

He brushed a kiss across her forehead, then gazed into her beautifully unique eyes. "It's nearly two, sweetheart. Maybe there is something we can do."

He glanced over his shoulder at Wally. "Andy and I have an appointment at Gene Mott's house and somehow, before we leave there today, we're going to learn the truth about his paralysis."

AFTER GIVING WALLY the task of driving to Virginia City to find out who held legal title to the Woodworths' old homestead, Andy and Jack set out for Gene Mott's house.

As they rounded the corner by the Golden Broom, Jack glanced down at Andy and his thoughts skipped to the feel of her beneath him, thoughts that tended to wipe the purpose of their mission right out of his mind. But the moment Andy gazed up at him, he saw again that she wasn't wearing her colored contacts. He liked her eyes best this way, but they made him acutely aware of who she was and just how much danger her very identity put her in.

Deciding he'd better concentrate on that, Jack reached for her hand, receiving and giving reassurance. Although she looked tense, Andy rewarded him with a grateful smile.

At the very end of Ruby Lane, one block below Duke Plummer's, sat Gene's house, a large one-story with the appearance of recent remodeling. The front yard was ringed with a short wrought-iron fence. They walked through the gate, past the small patch of clipped green lawn, stopping to examine the concrete walk that separated well-tended flower beds from the grass.

"The perfect walkway to accommodate a wheelchair-bound gardener," Jack whispered.

"If Gene isn't paraplegic, he's gone to a lot of trouble to keep up the sham." Andy's stomach ached with anxiety. She nodded to the wide ramp leading to the front veranda and another angled at the side of the house, apparently for access from a back door. "Who would keep up such a pretense for twenty years?"

"Someone who feared lifetime incarceration." Jack followed her to the front door. "Don't forget, he's built a successful career pretending to be a woman."

"But he could have moved away. Changed his name. Still had his career."

"Not with the threat of your returning one day to point the finger at him."

"I should think that would send him fleeing."

"No, sweetheart, fleeing would make him look guilty. Think about it. As long as he stayed here and made no effort to hide, made himself look helpless, gained people's sympathy and respect, how much of a threat could you be? Even if you did show up one day, it would be your word against a popular and wealthy man's. After all, you were only five years old. He'd probably sue you for defamation of character, claim—since you also write novels—that you were picking on him because of professional jealousy."

Impotent rage swirled inside Andy. "Are you saying he could get away with murdering my parents—even if I were to remember *he* was Nightmare Man?"

"Not as long as there's a breath in this body." Jack kissed her forehead. "What I'm saying is—don't let the props fool you."

Before Jack could knock, the door swung open.

"Thought I heard voices out here." Cliff, his face red, his

body slick with a fine film of sweat, wore only running shoes and jogging shorts. His white blond hair flopped over his forehead. His gaze immediately crawled over Andy, and as usual she wanted to slap him. He stepped aside, inviting them indoors. "Uncle and I have been working out."

"He invited us over." Andy glanced at her watch. Usually punctual to a fault, she saw they were ten minutes late. "Perhaps I got the time wrong?"

"No, he's expecting you."

Odd, Andy thought, that he'd schedule his workout for the same time he'd invited guests. Or was it calculated? Was this his way of controlling what he could of situations? Or did he want them to see him in his gym?

The entry smelled of lemon wax, and the oak floors gleamed as if recently polished. The interior was all clean lines and simple furnishings, giving the living room a spacious, tidy appearance. Gram would definitely have approved.

Cliff led them to the gym. The doorway was wide enough to oblige two wheelchairs side by side. Mirrors lined three of the walls, and the fourth held a plate-glass window overlooking Ruby Lane. No doubt he'd seen them coming.

Gene, his upper body—muscles bulging—clad in a tank top, his lower half in sweatpants, stood with his back to them. In the mirror Andy could see that his usually ghostly face was flushed as he held himself erect between parallel bars—the kind of thing used in physical therapy to help patients relearn to walk. Her heart hitched. Was Gene able to walk?

"Uncle!" Cliff cried, his voice ringing with alarm.

Gene jerked around, startled. His legs buckled and he dropped to the floor, his chin whacking one metal bar as he collapsed.

Chapter Fourteen

Andy and Jack had been gone an hour when Wally emerged from the motel cabin and started down the path for the parking lot. He hadn't wanted to worry them, but he'd felt a little light-headed before they left. This infernal heat. Sun beating down on these flat-roofed cabins. Hadn't Minna Kroft heard of air conditioning?

Of course, this darned heartburn didn't help. Too much caffeine. "Give it up," the doctor said. How the hell did he do that after fifty years? Doctors and their rules. He pulled in a deep breath. His short nap had brought back his equilibrium. Despite still being a bit tired from loss of sleep the night before, he felt, if not great, then good.

He palmed his car keys, noticing a slight tremor in his hand. Maybe "good" was too generous. He clasped the keys tighter. Nerves were shot. He was losing his edge. Getting old. And it annoyed the hell out of him. But maybe the nerves were to be expected—what with Junior and that sweet Miss Woodworth coming within a cat's hair of being killed.

But which of their suspects was Nightmare Man? The question stopped him. He ran a hand over his crew cut. There'd been something…something he'd meant to mention to Junior. Damn. What was it? Now that he thought about it—since last night after dinner in the hotel, something had been nagging him.

He'd seen something or someone in the hotel dining room
that reminded him eerily of Jack senior—or of the time right
around Jack senior's death. The heat seemed to evaporate the
breath from his lungs. He mopped his brow with his handkerchief and started walking again.

The inability to recall whatever it was exasperated him. He
kicked at a stone in his path, nearly striking a big, furry black
cat as it emerged from the underbrush. Wally drew a sharp
breath. The cat started, arched its back and glared at him.

"Sorry, fellah." Grinning at himself, Wally squatted to the
cat's level with the intention of making amends. Somehow
the cat looked familiar. "Say, do I know you?"

It struck him like a welcome breeze that this big black cat
with the stubby tail and yellow eyes looked like the one Karen
Bradley had described to her parents. *Outlaw.* He reached a
hand toward the cat, half expecting it to take off. Instead, it
rubbed its head against his knuckles. Wally grinned and
stroked the animal's head. "Friendly cuss, aren't you?"

It occurred to him then that he'd never gotten around to
asking Minna Kroft about Karen Bradley and her cat. Not that
it would matter much to anyone now, he supposed, except
perhaps the Bradleys. Hell, no wonder he'd lost his edge. He
was getting downright soft lately. Sentimental. Caring about
a bum like Gus Dillard. About complete strangers like the
Bradleys. But darn it all, his heart went out to them, suffering
as they were. If someone had killed his daughter Brandi…
Well, it would just rip his heart out, that's what.

Maybe Minna would tell him some nice anecdote about
Karen, something he could relate to her parents that would
ease their suffering, if only slightly. He scooped up the cat
and strolled into the motel office. Minna was nowhere to be
seen, but at the sound of the bell, she called out from somewhere in back, "Be right there."

The small office looked like a home for wayward cats.

Wally liked the animals, but this seemed a bit much. He wondered if they kept the widow company during the off-season.

Minna appeared from the hallway. One look at him holding the cat and her amber eyes shone with surprise and awe. "Satan don't usually take to strangers. You're a cat lover, aren't ya?"

Wally nodded, rubbing the purring feline under the jaw. "I used to have a big guy like this one." Maybe he should get another.

"Really?" Minna beamed. "Why don't ya come have some iced tea with me and tell me all about him?"

Wally glanced at his watch. It was still early and iced tea sounded great. He supposed he could spare a few minutes.

JACK AND CLIFF SPARED no haste reaching Gene. Andy stood to one side, horrified and frightened. They'd wanted proof that Gene Mott wasn't Nightmare Man. Well, they'd just gotten it.

"Didn't I warn you about trying that without me, Uncle? You're too worn out from yesterday afternoon's riding."

Gene rubbed his jaw where it had struck the bar. "I'm stronger than you give me credit for."

Cliff rolled his eyes behind his uncle's back.

"Just get me in my chair."

Jack reached to help Cliff, but Gene shrank from him as though he didn't like being touched. "Cliff and I can manage."

Jack stepped back.

Andy watched Cliff fuss over his uncle in a way that reminded her of a…nurse? Of course. Why hadn't she realized sooner? A would-be stud like old Cliffie could hardly be satisfied hanging out year-round in this small town waiting for the summers and the influx of young women. He wasn't here for the fun of it. He was a paid companion and male nurse for his uncle. Despite his obvious faults, Andy found herself thinking better of him.

Once in his chair, Gene lifted one leg, then the other, onto the footrests.

Jack leaned against the wall, glanced out the window overlooking the front walk, then back at Gene, trying to figure out if the fall had been staged for their benefit, timed to their arrival. Or had it been genuine? "Must be some procedure getting you on a horse, Gene."

"It's not as complicated as you seem to imagine." Twin spots of peach dotted Gene's snowy cheeks, the color as unnatural on his ghoulish face as rouge on a corpse. But what had caused the blush—the fall or Jack's impudence? Gene lifted his chin; a red welt adorned a small area just above his jawline. "The stable has a ramp that puts me level with the horse's back and my upper body, as you can see, is quite strong."

"Still," Jack persisted, "it must require some assistance?"

Gene seemed to be having trouble regaining his breath. Or was he just angry and having trouble regaining his inner calm? "A little. Why the curiosity about my riding abilities, Jack? I thought you'd accompanied Ms. Hart here so she could see my diaries." Gene turned his cool blue eyes on Andrea. "Or should I call you, Ms. Woodworth?"

Andy had known this was coming and was braced for it. Nonetheless, the chilly eeriness of his eyes sent a shiver down her spine. "Why not…Andy?"

"As you wish." He glanced back at Jack.

Jack dropped his gaze to Gene's legs. Were they as wasted as they seemed in the baggy sweatpants or were the pants baggy to hide solid, muscled legs? If only Gene had let him help Cliff lift him into his chair, he'd have known for sure. As it was, he couldn't believe the evidence of his own eyes. Couldn't be certain the fall hadn't been staged.

"And how about you, Jack?" Gene's voice sliced through his dark suspicions. "Is Black your real name?"

Jack raised his gaze to Gene's. "A stage name. But you can still call me Jack." If Gene wasn't going to pull his punches, neither was Jack. "You and Duke looked like you'd been doing something more strenuous than riding yesterday. How'd you both get so dirty and sweaty?"

"Ah. Now all is clear." Gene laughed without mirth. "We'd been racing—as fast as the horses could carry us across a very dusty field. Riding that fast is one of the few physical pleasures I can still enjoy."

Jack pressed his lips together. Gene's answer was plausible. Pity diluted Jack's suspicions. He understood the pleasure of riding a stallion at breakneck speed. He'd gotten dirty and sweaty plenty of times himself doing just that.

"Perhaps we should let Gene get some rest after his fall," Andy said, gazing at Jack. "I can always see the diaries another day."

Gene raised a hand in protest. "Nonsense. I insist."

He shooed Cliff away. "I can manage. Why don't you go shower?"

Cliff shrugged. "Sure. See you in a few." He spun on his heel and disappeared through the doorway.

"Please follow me." Gene set the wheelchair in gear and led them out of the gym and through the living room to the back of the house.

Here, double wide doors accessed an office any writer would kill for. One long wall was solid bookshelves, another displayed poster-sized photos of his book covers, a third was all window and looked out toward the Madison Mountain Range. The view stole Andy's breath with its vividness.

"The diaries are on the desk." Gene pointed to the massive oak desk that sat in the center of the room. There was no chair, just a clear floor mat on the pale green carpet. His desk, much like her own in Seattle, supported a computer and a laser printer, several books and a closed folder that likely contained a manuscript in progress. File cabinets occupied the same wall as the doorway.

Andy shifted her large purse across her shoulders. With all the uproar of the past few days, writing had been put on a back burner. Even if she had really come here just to peruse the diaries, she'd never be able to concentrate on her book. Not until this was behind her. The sudden realization that she wasn't going to meet her deadline for the first time ever added another tier of distress to her already overloaded nerves.

She started toward the desk, but froze, her muscles tensing, her mouth drying as her attention snagged on one of the framed posters. It depicted a giant bird claw on a solid black background with each talon tipped in red. Like blood. Without looking around at Gene, she willed her stomach to settle and asked, "How did you get interested in horror?"

"Probably the way most horror writers started—as a fan of Stephen King's. Reading his stories not only gave me pleasure but triggered my imagination. The old 'what if.' And I found myself coming up with a new twist here, a new twist there."

Andy had read one or two of his "twists," and in her opinion Stephen King had nothing to fear from Gene Mott, even though his books were recently—upon release—all automatically hitting the New York bestseller lists.

She turned to face Gene, aware of Jack's presence, gaining courage from his presence. "Did you know my father?"

The switch of subjects didn't seem to bother Gene. "Everyone who grew up in this town knew your father. I considered him a friend."

"You never married." Jack dropped the statement like a bombshell, but the only one it seemed to affect was Andy.

She glanced at him as he moved beside her, wondering why he'd asked this particular question, but his silvery green eyes weren't giving anything away.

Gene also glanced at Jack and moved his chair closer to

them. "No, Jack. The only woman I ever loved, loved another. An old story, no longer sad, just tedious."

Andy's heartbeat accelerated as she instantly understood Jack's motive: he was trying to find out if Gene had also been smitten with her mother. It was all she could do to keep from asking the woman's name.

Sunlight reached in through the picture window and glinted off something hanging from the steering knob of the wheelchair. Andy's gaze went to the source of the reflection and her stomach dropped to her toes. It appeared to be a golden three-pronged hook of some kind—very like whatever had been used to slice her wrist. Her right hand covered her left wrist where Gram's bracelet now banded, yet didn't conceal, the old scar. She pointed at the object. "W-what's that?"

"What, this?" He lifted the object from its perch and held it out. "It belongs on my key ring. It was a gift from Cliff— a raven's claw he had bronzed for me after my book *The Raven's Claw* made the *New York Times* list. It was the first book to hit the list and my biggest thrill."

"It even opens beer bottles," Cliff boasted, striding into the room wearing faded jeans and a white T-shirt advertising the Bud Light Bowl, his hair damp from showering. He carried a beer bottle to his uncle and let Gene demonstrate.

"Can I get anyone else a beer?"

Jack shook his head. "Not me."

"No," Andy said. "We're meeting someone for supper soon."

Gene nodded. "Then you'd probably like to get started on those diaries. Cliff, I'd like my own shower now. Then a nap. You two just make yourselves at home. Next time we meet, I hope to be in better mettle."

"I'll be back in a while," Cliff said, then followed his uncle from the room.

The moment they were gone, Jack pulled Andy against him. "How you holding up, sweetheart?"

"I'm fine." *As long as you're here with me.* She returned his hug, then gazed up at him. "What do you think?"

"I think Gene's either one of the world's greatest undiscovered actors or he's exactly what he seems. But it wouldn't hurt to give this room a quick once-over."

Andy agreed. Jack tackled the file cabinets, she the desk. Minutes later he perched one hip on the edge of the desk. "Find anything?"

She shook her head. "You?"

"A lot of correspondence with editors and other authors. A folder full of old rejections. Tax records."

"None of which is unusual for a writer. The desk has stamps, and paper, and pens and pencils and a phone book." Andy noticed then that Jack was holding a folder. She gazed up at him, her pulse picking up its beat. "What's that?"

"I found this in the bottom drawer—at the back. It contains a set of old X rays."

Jack carried the folder to the window, then held up the X ray. It was dated some twenty years earlier and showed a spinal column with a hairline crack near the base. Andy said, "Proof positive."

"Yeah." Jack tucked the X ray back in the folder.

Footsteps coming down the hall sent them scurrying— Andy back to the desk, Jack to replace the folder in the file cabinet. Cliff came into the room just as Jack was recrossing to the desk. The phone rang and as Cliff picked up his step to reach it, Andy and Jack said they'd let themselves out.

Minutes later they were headed back down the hill toward Main Street. Wally was meeting them in the hotel shortly to compare notes. "Well," Jack said. "Now we know Gene Mott isn't Nightmare Man."

Andy caught hold of his hand and smiled up at him, feeling encouraged for the first time in days. "We've finally taken one step closer to finding him. Nightmare Man is either Red

Yager or Duke Plummer. And I'll bet one of them holds the deed on my parents' old homestead.''

It was odd, Andy mused. Gram hadn't been in her thoughts the whole time she'd been at Mott's, but suddenly she felt her presence with such force—and with it came an inexplicable anxiety, knotting her stomach. It was as if Gram were trying to warn her. About what? Was it because now that they'd narrowed their field of suspects they were in even greater danger? Or was it something specific?

WALLY SPOTTED JACK and Andy coming down the hill from Ruby Lane as he drove along Main Street. Jack seemed absorbed in conversation with the comely Miss Woodworth, totally unaware of traffic on Main Street. Junior seemed smitten.

Talking to Minna Kroft had moved him no closer to solving the mystery of who the killer was, but at least he now had a sweet tale to carry home to two grieving parents. And, by thunder, he felt better about that.

Besides, two hours with Minna Kroft, drinking her tea, chatting, had oddly relaxed him. Maybe it was the tea she'd served him. Chamomile. Didn't that have some kind of soothing properties? Seemed to have worked on him. Even his jitters were gone.

Virginia City was mere minutes from Alder Gulch. He parked beside the Madison County Courthouse, hurried inside and located the records department. A slender woman in her late forties stood behind the counter. When she saw him, her face pulled as tight as the knot of brown hair on the crown of her head. She gathered her purse to her. ''We're closed. You'll have to come back tomorrow. We're open at 10 a.m.''

Wally put on his best dimpled grin and strolled right up to her counter, digging his wallet from his pocket. He laid it open-faced on the counter, his press credentials in full view. ''I'm Wallingford Lester, editor in chief of the *Butte Sun*. I'm on an explosive story—an exclusive that will put this county on the tongues of American citizens from New York to L.A. It's set to roll in tomorrow's edition, but I'm missing a key fact before we can go to print. Please, this can't wait until tomorrow. I've got a whole staff waiting for my call—and I only need you to look up one little fact.''

''Well, I—''

''I'll be sure to mention your name and how cooperative *you* were, Miss...?''

That did the trick. She bit hook, line and sinker and he could tell this was the most exciting thing that had happened in this woman's life in a long time. The tight look vanished and her face became more animated with every question she asked trying to get him to tell her about the ''explosive story.'' With some fast sidestepping he managed to avoid giving her specific answers.

Half an hour later he possessed photocopies of the legal titles. Excitement robbed him of a few degrees of his calm and his hand once again trembled. He'd have to hightail it back to Alder Gulch to meet Junior and Miss Woodworth for supper so as not to worry them.

What he'd discovered was damned interesting. Mopping at his brow and grinning, he hustled out to his car, flopped the papers on the front seat beside him and started the engine. Yessir, yessir. It wasn't the present owners of the land that had caught his attention, but the owner before them. Had Andy and Jack had as much good luck as he'd had?

As he left Virginia City, the weird nagging he'd not been able to put his finger on attacked him anew, prickling the fine hair on the nape of his neck. God, he was getting edgy again and he couldn't account for it. He peered into the rearview mirror, half expecting to find someone following him, but the only vehicle on the road was his.

He'd hardly gone another mile when the feeling of being followed swept him again.

He chided himself for a fool. But his gaze went unbidden

to the mirror. Instead of empty road, two burning eyes peered back at him from the rear seat. Wally gasped, nearly jumping out of his skin. The car swerved. He felt cold steel against his throat. Not a knife, but something three-pronged that cut into his flesh as if it were soft butter. "W-w-what do you want?"

"Pull over."

"Yes," Wally croaked. Immediately he tapped the brake and steered for the shoulder. His face burned with heat and his pulse thundered through his veins, roaring in his ears. His chest felt as if a band were throttling it. Alder Gulch was around the next bend, but this section of road was uninhabited. Totally deserted at the moment.

Again his gaze went to the mirror, and in that instant he finally remembered. The night Jack senior was killed, he'd seen these same burning eyes looking in the window of his car as he'd pulled from the newspaper parking lot.

Dear God, he knew who Nightmare Man was. He'd known all along. White-hot rage ripped through Wally, overriding his pain. If he was going to die, it wouldn't be alone. Nor in vain. He rammed his foot down on the gas pedal and aimed the car for the ditch.

Chapter Fifteen

The town remained tourist-free, and an eerie hush hung over it as hot and oppressive as the unrelenting sun beating down on Andy, reminding her that a murderer, who was intent on adding her to his list of victims, walked these streets. She shivered in the heat. How had she ever thought this town was welcoming her? What it had been doing was lying in wait for her return.

Few patrons occupied the dining room of the Golden Broom. Andy and Jack chose a private corner table and ordered beer to wet their parched throats. Jack glanced around, spotting the sheriff and a couple of his deputies at a table across the room. But his curiosity leaned toward who was missing. "I wonder where Red is?"

Andy hadn't been able to shake the foreboding she'd felt earlier. "I don't know, but I'd feel better if I knew where both of our suspects were and what they were up to."

Both. Jack pulled off his Stetson and finger-combed his hair. She still refused to consider Minna Kroft a suspect. He wished he felt as certain of the woman's innocence. "And what's keeping Wally?"

"Why don't you go see if he's coming down the road?"

Jack immediately sprang from his chair and headed for the swinging bar doors. Wally was a punctual man, but now that

Jack thought about it, he'd looked more tired than usual. Was the heat too much for him?

As Jack neared the door, two familiar voices drifted in from just beyond the opening. Cliff and Minna. They seemed to be...arguing? Slowing to a halt, Jack stayed out of sight and listened.

"Ya swear to me ya didn't try shootin' 'em?"

"Why would I do that?"

"Ya know darned tootin' why."

"Are you nuts? I wouldn't kill someone for that."

"Well, sure as we're standin' here, somebody gave it a danged good try."

"You're serious?" There was incredulity in Cliff's voice. "Someone tried killing them?"

Minna didn't answer, but Jack could almost see her head nodding, her fluffy gray hair waving. Then she said, "And ya know where they stayed the night? In the mine, that's where."

Cliff groaned. "And now that friend of theirs is at the courthouse."

"I told ya as much."

Jack stepped through the bar doors. Cliff and Minna jerked toward him. Fear whizzed through their eyes, but they both recovered quickly enough that if Jack hadn't heard their conversation, he might have convinced himself he'd imagined the looks. "Cliff, your uncle feeling better?"

"Huh? Oh, sure, he's napping."

"Good. Why don't you and Minna come on in and let me buy you both a beer?"

Cliff gave Minna a nervous glance. "That's all right, I really should get back to Uncle."

Jack laughed. "Hell, he'll probably be okay long enough for you to swallow a bottle of brew."

Cliff started shaking his head. But Jack wasn't taking no for an answer. Gently he caught them both by the arm and led them inside and over to the table where Andy sat alone.

Andy frowned, started to ask what was going on, but caught Jack's slight shaking of his head and recovered quickly. "Well, hello again, Cliff. Minna."

Small talk ruled the conversation until everyone had a beer in front of them. Then Jack sprang. "Minna, why don't you tell us what reason ole Cliffie here might have for killing Andy and me?"

Cliff spit beer across the table. Minna's face turned beet red. Andy stiffened. "What?"

"Tell her what, Cliff." Jack's voice was low with menace.

Cliff glared at him. "I don't have to tell you anything."

Minna sighed. "Give it up, boy. Yer holdin' a losin' hand. They'll know soon enough."

Cliff jerked his head, flipping a hank of his hair out of his eyes. His expression was nervous and guilty.

Jack started to stand. "I had a bad night and my temper is shorter than a disturbed diamondback right about now. Give Andy her answer."

Cliff swallowed over his Adam's apple. "It's nothing, really. Just that since Minna told me Andy is really Lee Lee Woodworth and that her parents once owned a piece of land I recently purchased, I was afraid maybe she'd have some...some claim to the...to anything that might be found on the property."

"Like in the old mine?"

"Yeah."

"And why would this involve Minna."

"Well, she sort of put up half the cash for the place."

"And you've been working the mine in your spare time?"

"Yeah. But I haven't had much of that."

"How long have you owned the property?"

"Since this winter."

"Who'd you buy it from?"

Before Cliff could answer, Red Yager slammed open the bar doors and ran inside. His rust-colored mustache twitched and his head bobbed as he scanned the room. "Sheriff! Thank God. There's been an accident. Just down the road. Some poor guy's smashed up his car. It looks real bad."

Jack felt an inexplicable tightening around his heart. As the sheriff and his deputies scrambled to their feet, he did the same and was at Red's side without knowing how he'd gotten there. He interrupted the sheriff's questions. "What kind of car, Red?"

Jack noticed a welt forming above Red's left eye.

Red squinted at him. "An old blue Bronco."

Wally's car. Ice flowed over Jack's heart. He swore. "Where?"

Red explained. Jack was moving toward the door when Andy caught up to him. She grasped his arm. Her heart was in her throat. "What?"

"Wally."

"Oh, no." Her stomach churned and her head felt light. She'd known something awful was going to happen, but somehow, she'd imagined it would be to Jack or herself. "Was it really an accident?"

"I don't know. This heat hasn't been doing him any good, nor has the stress." Panic robbed Jack of his reasoning skills. "I'm going with the sheriff and find out."

"I'll go, too."

If this was as bad as Red indicated, Jack wanted to spare Andy the horror. "I don't think that's a good idea. It might be pretty awful. Why don't you go back to the motel? I'll have Birdsill send one of his deputies with you."

Andy didn't want to be parted from Jack, but if what he said about Wally was true, she didn't want to see it. Besides, he'd let her know as soon as possible what was happening. "Don't bother the sheriff. I'll be safe with Minna."

Jack had to admit his worries about Minna being Nightmare Man had disappeared when she'd accused Cliff of yesterday's attack on them. "All right. I'll let you know what's going on the minute I have news."

"I'll be praying for Wally."

But Jack knew as soon as he arrived at the crash site and saw the sheriff's expression that Andy's prayers for Wally would be too late.

The sheriff shook his head. "I'm afraid he's dead."

"What happened?" Awful pain plunged through Jack "How?"

"Did he have any heart problems?"

Jack nodded. "He was taking pills for high blood pressure."

"As county coroner I've seen my share of heart attacks and my initial examination tells me this might just be another Probably came on sudden and killed him instantly. We'l know more after the autopsy."

At least he hadn't been shot—like Virgil, Jack thought finding little comfort in the knowledge. He gave Birdsill the names and telephone numbers for Wally's next of kin, ther stood to one side, numb, while the ambulance arrived and took the body away to a funeral home in Virginia City.

How many times had he covered auto crashes for the *Sun* After the first horrendous time, he'd always remained detached, his reporter's instincts taking hold and carrying him through. Not now. Nothing about Wally could be handled impersonally. But his affection for Wally was getting in the way of making certain death had occurred naturally—and he owed it to his old friend to prove that.

Studying the outside of the Bronco told him nothing. He moved around to the open driver's door and stuck his head inside. The engine had been rammed into the dashboard and the steering wheel was bent, but neither sported so much as a trace of blood—which might mean that Wally had beer dead before the Bronco hit the telephone pole, just like the sheriff thought. Jack sighed.

As to what Wally might have discovered at the courthouse, he'd apparently brought nothing tangible with him. It didn't matter, anyway. They had learned who owned the property without Wally's help. The possibility that he'd sent his old friend to his death—for no reason—weighed heavily on Jack.

Someone tapped him on the shoulder. He jolted and bumped his head on the doorframe.

"Hey, fellah. You need some help?"

Slowly withdrawing from the Bronco, Jack gazed at the stranger, whose apparel screamed "tourist." Across the road two minivans were parked one before the other, both full to the rear windows with kids and travel gear.

The stranger repeated his offer of help. Jack thanked him, explained the situation and sent the man and his traveling companions on their way. More vehicles were coming down the road and Jack realized Birdsill must have lifted the ban on tourism sometime last night. If he didn't leave now, others would be stopping, asking him questions.

He started to shut the Bronco door when his gaze fell on a dark spot on the back of the driver's seat. Reaching inside, he touched it. It was drying rapidly, but a spot of red moisture adhered to his fingertip. Sniffing, he detected the unmistakable coppery scent of blood.

His instincts kicked in like a slam to the gut. If Wally had died from a heart attack, why was there fresh blood on this seat? A cursory search revealed nothing sharp enough to puncture flesh. His skin prickled. This needed looking into before an autopsy was performed.

Jack ran back through town, dodging the new influx of foot traffic as he raced to the motel. Andy was in Minna's apartment. He told them Wally was dead, eschewing any mention of the sheriff's theory that it had been a heart attack.

Minna blanched at the news and dropped into her chair, visibly shaken. "But he was here not more than an hour or so ago, drinkin' tea, talkin' 'bout cats. Whew! The Lord likes His surprises, don't He?''

"Maybe."

Jack's odd response jerked Andy's curiosity, but as her gaze rose to his, she saw a pain in his eyes that overwhelmed any other concern. He looked much the same way she'd felt when Gram had died. She went to him and folded her arms around his lean waist. "I'm so sorry, Jack."

Jack wrapped his arms around Andy, amazed that holding her somehow lessened the pain in his heart. But nothing could lessen his need to get to Virginia City. Or his need to get Andy alone and tell her what he suspected. However, it went against his nature to leave another human being in such obvious distress as Minna was in now. "Maybe Minna would like some tea?"

"I think this calls fer somethin' stiffer," Minna said. "The brandy's there in the hutch. Jack looks like he could use a jolt of it, too."

"No, thanks." Jack released Andy and stood tensely to one side, watching her pour brandy into a small glass. As she carried the drink to Minna, he said, "I'm going to the funeral home in Virginia City to…make arrangements, Andy. I thought you might like to come along."

For the first time Andy realized something besides natural shock and grief had Jack agitated, and by now she knew him well enough to understand he wanted to tell her whatever it was in private. But there was something more in his look, an emotion so powerful it joined her to him in some intangible way that could not be explained or analyzed, but that went right to the core of her being as if he'd left his brand on her soul. "Of course."

Minna licked brandy from her lips and nodded. "And don't you two worry 'bout me. I'll be jest fine."

A family was heading into the motel office as they left.

When they were in his pickup truck headed for Virginia

City, Jack told her about the blood on the seat. "I'm not going to the funeral home to make any arrangements. His family will do that after the autopsy. What I want is a look at Wally now."

They rounded the bend, coming upon the old blue Bronco, its crumpled nose kissing a telephone pole. Cringing, Andy looked away as they drove past it. "I'll be right beside you."

He reached out and covered her hand. "Are you sure?"

Looking at dead bodies would never make her list of ten favorite things to do, but Jack needed her and that need gave her courage. Besides, she could almost hear Gram telling her it was important. "Yes, I'm sure, but what about Birdsill? After what he said this morning about our staying out of his investigation, he isn't likely to appreciate this."

"Birdsill doesn't think this *is* part of his investigation. He believes Wally died of heart failure." Jack glanced at her. "But you're right. There's no sense rousing his wrath without cause. Do you think you could distract the funeral director long enough for me to get to Wally?"

"I'll give it my best shot."

Jack squeezed her hand. Strange to think he'd met this woman only days ago, and yet he could think of no one else he'd want sharing this awful time with him.

They drove the rest of the way in silence, slowing as they reached the city limits, and maneuvered the streets until they came to the establishment they sought. Built on a knoll, the funeral home reminded Andy of a one-story house with a windowless basement. The top level, sun-bleached red with faded gray trim, sported several smoky opaque windows and a ramp leading to an entrance of double doors. The basement was made of unpainted concrete blocks.

The only vehicle parked in the designated area was a black hearse of vintage age. Jack pulled his pickup next to it and turned off the motor. "Are you ready?"

Ignoring the tremors in her stomach, Andy nodded. While

Jack searched for an entrance to the basement, she strolled in through the front doors and found herself in a long, wide foyer. Muzak floated from some unseen source and the sickly sweet smell of too many flowers jammed into one room filled her nostrils. She pressed a fist against her unsettled stomach and called loudly, "Hello, is anyone here?"

Footsteps sounded; someone ascending stairs preceded the opening and banging of a door at the end of the foyer. A wiry little man with a pasty complexion hurried toward her buttoning the top button of his short-sleeved white shirt.

"Mrs. Driggs, you're early." His voice was high-pitched, his smile overly solicitous.

Andy didn't bother to correct him. His mistaking her for someone else was better than any of the lies that had popped into her head. Praying the real Mrs. Driggs wouldn't show up any time soon, she sputtered, "I, I—"

"Oh, I understand. Your aunt is ready for you. I followed your instructions to the letter and everything's all set up." He gestured for her to come into a room directly off the foyer. "Right in here."

The room looked like a small chapel full of empty pews with a pulpit at the front. Flower arrangements possessed every inch of floor, their colliding fragrances cloying in the compact space, churning Andy's stomach more than ever. She froze, her gaze riveted on the front of the room, on an open casket and the pasty profile of its occupant.

"She turned out quite lovely if I do say so myself," the mortician said. "Now, I'll just leave you alone with your grief."

"No!" The word came out as a yelp and Andy felt her face warming. She reached out for the little man. "Please, I have an awful headache—the heat, you know. Could I trouble you for an aspirin and a glass of water?"

JACK HAD NO TROUBLE finding the side door, and his fears of it being locked vanished as he realized it was slightly ajar.

Apparently the ambulance drivers or someone else hadn't completely shut it. He stepped inside, immediately feeling as if he'd stepped from summer into winter; the room was dark and gloomy and cold. The stench of formaldehyde hit his nostrils, and his stomach lurched.

Wally lay stretched on a gurneylike table looking as if he'd fallen asleep. His clothes were half-removed, as though the task had been interrupted. It made Jack more aware than ever how little time he had. Even now, Andy might be running out of ways to engage the mortician.

The second his eyes adjusted to the change in light, Jack spotted the wound on Wally's neck—three small punctures as if some deformed, three-fanged vampire had bitten him. The ache of loss in Jack's chest pressed more heavily. He leaned closer, realizing with a quickening pulse that the gap between each puncture was bone-chillingly close to the span between each of the three scars on Andy's wrist. Maybe exactly the same.

He was back in the pickup when she came down the front stoop of the funeral home. Her face was the color of bleached flour. She told him the funny, awful story of her deception as Jack drove out of town.

"You did well." He chuckled, then grew sober. "I found what I was looking for. Someone else was in the car with Wally."

Andy drew a shaky breath. "Nightmare Man?"

Jack nodded. "Who else?"

"But why?" She chewed thoughtfully on a snagged cuticle. "What did Wally know that he hadn't told us?"

"I've been wrestling with that question, but the only thing I can come up with would be something he might have found out about the Flying W, and we can't check with the clerk until tomorrow."

"Oh, Jack, I forgot to tell you." Andy sat straighter and

gazed up at him. "Minna said Cliff and she got the idea to buy my parents' old homestead from Duke after he told them Red Yager had bought the place as soon as he could—after Gram and I disappeared—for the cost of the land taxes. So Red knew darn good and well that I didn't still hold the claim to the land."

"No wonder Minna gave him such an odd look."

"That's not all. Apparently he made enough money off the mine to do the original remodel on the Golden Broom."

"Well, I'll be damned."

Alder Gulch loomed ahead, looking more like the first time Andy had seen it—the street full of foot traffic, vehicles of various makes and models wearing licenses from several different states parked everywhere.

Jack broke into her thoughts. "Red arrived on the accident site awfully fast, and he had a welt forming above his left eye."

"We'd better talk to him again."

"Damned straight."

Andy could see he was still shell-shocked at the loss of his friend, and more than anything she ached to comfort him. She spoke softly, reaching her hand to his thigh. "Take me back to the motel and just hold me for a while?"

Jack nodded, pulled her close and kissed her forehead.

NIGHTMARE MAN GAZED into the mirror at the bump rising on his forehead. It was small, more red than purple, tender to the touch and close enough to his hairline that it probably wouldn't draw attention. An insidious ache tweaked his temples, but he wasn't sure if it was from the bump he'd taken or from losing his temper.

Only now, was he calming down. At first he'd felt cheated—not being able to end the editor's life in his elected fashion. On further reflection, he felt that things couldn't have turned out better. The sheriff might wonder at the three puncure wounds on the editor's neck, but an autopsy would prove he old man died of natural causes.

He crossed the room, removed the scrapbook from its secret hiding place and laid it open on the floor. Kneeling, he stuck he papers he'd taken from the front seat of Wally's Bronco onto a blank page and hand-ironed them flat.

A shiver scurried down his spine as he remembered the odd gleam of recognition in the editor's eyes. Had he been an unknown threat all these years—a wild card? Well, that was one danger eliminated. A cold chuckle died in his throat. He closed the album and tucked it away.

There was only one danger left: the worrisome Ms. Woodworth. But in a few hours she would join her friend, the editor, in hell. The thought of his bold plan set his pulse zipping like hot water through his veins. Soon little Lee Lee would haunt his dreams no longer.

Chapter Sixteen

Jack realized the moment he wrapped both arms around Andy that merely holding her would not be enough, that merely kissing her would not cleanse from them the evil that had held them in its grasp and brought them to their emotional knees.

But as they made love on the small bed in his cabin, every intimate touch of hers renewed his spirit, reminding him how very alive he was, how very vital, and he surrendered to her tender machinations, feasting on her offerings, giving in return with equal generosity.

Afterward, he felt whole again—still saddened by Wally's death, still angry, but restored in his dedication to bring the murderer to justice.

Andy knew she ought to be exhausted. Instead, she felt rejuvenated—connecting with Jack in this most intimate of ways had somehow revitalized every cell in her body. She lay naked in his arms, his flesh cleaving to hers as she snuggled against his chest. In a perfect world she could stay like this forever.

But there was nothing perfect about their situation. Jack's friend had been murdered. Virgil Cooper, too. They had to figure out who Nightmare Man was. And soon. She gazed up at Jack. His sage green eyes held the dazed afterglow of their lovemaking, but there was also a touch of sadness and a hint of fear. She hated that hint of fear, knowing it was in large part for her. Because of her.

He stroked her hair away from her cheek. "I think we should go see Duke and Red. The sooner the better."

"Okay." She shoved up and away from Jack. What he'd suggested was necessary, but it shouldn't be. The power to end this suffering, to end this whole awful predicament, was locked inside her head. She wanted to scream. Why was she so terrified of remembering? Didn't she love Jack enough to trust that she would survive the horrendous memory?

The direction of this thought sobered her, chasing the last vestiges of afterglow as far from the forefront of her mind as the face of the man she could not recall. She scooted off the bed. "I'm going to take a shower."

Jack sat on the bed staring at the bathroom door for long minutes after Andy had shut it. The water was running and he considered going in to join her, to hold her again and embrace the safe cocoon of her love for as long as he could. But that would put off the inevitable, and he had the inexplicable sense that they couldn't spare the time.

Someone knocked on the cabin door. Jack jerked toward it, reaching for his jeans. "Who is it?"

"Cliff Mott."

"I'm coming." Jack buttoned his jeans as he crossed the room. He opened the door and leaned against it, scowling at Cliff. "Your uncle still napping?"

Cliff gave an arrogant toss of his head, flipping the ever-dangling lock of hair from his forehead. "He's working on his new book. I'm not welcome in the house when he's working. Look, I heard that fellah that died in the car crash was a friend of yours. I'm real sorry, man."

"Thanks." Jack swallowed hard over the lump of grief that was still too fresh and began shutting the door.

"Wait." Cliff jammed his foot between the frame and the door. "That's not the only reason I'm here. We're doing a special performance tonight.'' He glanced at his watch. ''In half an hour.''

Jack groaned. *No. He and Andy were going to question Red and Duke.* Inexplicably, the sense that they were running out of time mushroomed. ''Tell them to use my understudy to-night.''

Cliff shook his head. ''Can't. He went into Butte yesterday afternoon before Birdsill lifted the tourist ban and he hasn't come back or called. No one knows where he is. Unless he's seen a paper, he probably thinks the ban is still on.''

Jack sighed, frustration lassoing him like rope around a rodeo calf. ''Okay. I'll be there.''

''Be where?'' Andy asked, coming out of the bathroom as Jack shut the door on Cliff.

He explained as he laid a clean black shirt and jeans on the bed, then returned to the dresser for underwear.

''All right.'' Andy towel-dried her hair. ''I'll come watch the performance and we can question Duke and Red imme-diately afterward.''

''No.'' Jack stopped on his way to the bathroom and glanced over his shoulder. ''I don't want you on the street— getting 'accidentally' shot like Virgil Cooper.''

A chill went through Andy. She wasn't the only one who risked getting shot during the performance. ''What about you?''

''I'll keep my eyes open and my head down.''

Her heart clenched, but somehow she managed to keep the fear from her voice. ''I'll stay with Minna. She can handle a rifle well enough to keep me safe. That way you can concen-trate on keeping yourself safe, instead of worrying about me. I'll concentrate on remembering.''

Jack considered for a long moment, then nodded. ''Okay, but you have to promise you won't act on anything you might remember unless I'm at your side. Promise?''

The burden to remember bore down on her more heavily

than ever. Why couldn't she remember? Not doing so had dragged them into worse and worse jeopardy and even cost others their lives. "I promise."

"Not even if you remember something so vital it threatens to drive you up the wall?"

She rolled her eyes. "I don't have a death wish, you know."

He kissed the tip of her nose and gave her a look that warmed her heart. Andy stared after him as he moved into the bathroom and shut the door. Where was this going? Jack seemed to genuinely love her, but was it the kind of love that lasted a lifetime? Or one of those wildfire romances she'd heard girlfriends talk about that happened in a blinding flash, sweeping one into a swirl of passion and need, only to burn itself out as quickly as it began?

Her heart fluttered at this possibility, but she could not deny that what she felt for Jack had begun the second she'd laid eyes on him, nor that it had exploded into something fiery within days. Would it burn itself out the moment they captured their parents' murderer? Would she survive Nightmare Man only to lose the first man she had ever loved?

She jerked as if she'd been struck in the spine. Was that why she couldn't remember? Because once she did she might lose Jack forever? The thought of spending the rest of her life without him ripped through her like a jagged, dull-edged knife, tearing out her very desire to live. She dropped onto the bed. Dear God, it was true—and people had died because of the terrible fear that gripped her.

She rubbed her face with her damp palm. It was too late for Coop and Wally, but she would remember before someone else died.

Half an hour later as she paced Minna's living room, Andy still struggled with guilt, racking her brain, trying to remember. Minna brought her a mug of coffee, but Andy felt too jittery to even hold the mug.

Minna insisted, pressing it into her hands. "Drink it down, girl. Ya can't get yer mind to cooperate when yer tryin' so hard. It'll come back to ya when ya least expect it. Jest think 'bout somethin' else. Say, yer book."

Her book? All *that* reminded her of was how late it would be. But Minna did have a point. All this pressing to remember was giving her a headache. She accepted the coffee and sank to the sofa, disturbing the big Persian cat as the cushions jostled. It glanced at her disdainfully, then closed its eyes again.

Andy hugged the coffee mug to her chest. "I know I'm trying too hard. But it's so important."

"It'll—" The bell on the motel office door tinkled, cutting off Minna's words. She jerked toward the noise. "Customers. Now, you stay put and drink yer coffee. This shouldn't take more than ten minutes. I'll be back before ya know it."

As soon as Minna had gone, Andy set the mug on the end table and her gaze wandered to the bookshelf. Her spirits sank to an all-time low. She really should call her agent and tell him to contact her editor about an extension on the book. She rose and crossed the room to the telephone.

She grasped the receiver and lifted her finger to dial. The telephone was not a Touch-Tone but a rotary dial the same as the phone had been at the Flying W Ranch when she was five years old.

Without warning, her mind thrust her back to the night of her parents' deaths. She was five years old again. Tears she didn't want to cry filled her eyes and felt hot on her cheeks as she poked her finger into the rotary wheel at the big O and started to drag the dial around. Someone stepped from the shadows of the dining room.

Lee Lee jerked her head up and sucked in her breath. Nightmare Man. He was holding something that looked like a giant bird claw. His clothes were splattered with blood. And—she could see his face as clearly as if the man had stepped from the shadows of her mind into some bright spotlight.

Her stomach lurched.

"Hello, Lee Lee." The voice sounded so real, so close to her that Andy blinked.

The picture in her mind vanished. She was standing in Minna's living room, but she was no longer alone. Her blood ran cold. Someone had joined her. Nightmare Man. His face older now, but still so recognizable. Terror grabbed her chest, squeezing the air from her lungs. No scream would come.

Nightmare Man took a step toward her.

She dropped the phone. It clanked on the floor as she darted for the hallway. He jumped into her path and grasped her upper arm. Before she could cry out, Andy felt cold steel bite into her neck. She moaned as it cut her, spurting blood onto his shirt.

"I don't want to kill you here, but I will if I have to." He held her against his chest and growled the words in her ear.

Andy realized the only chance she might have of escaping was to buy some time. If only she could warn Jack, or get Minna's attention. But as Nightmare Man tugged her by the hair and the throat to the parking lot, she saw Minna leading a family toward one of the cabins on the knoll.

"Stop him." For half a second she thought someone was coming down Main Street to her rescue. But the shout was followed by another. "Stop him. He's stolen the orphans' fund."

Andy knew then that the shoot-out was just beginning and Jack would not be rescuing her. Her whole body trembled and tears burned her eyes. Frantically she struggled to hold on to her sanity, to stave off the terror.

Nightmare Man shoved her into her Cherokee. "You drive."

"I d-don't have my keys."

"I do." He dangled her key ring from one finger.

Feeling as if her heart would explode, Andy started the engine and pulled to the edge of Main Street.

"W-where?" It was the only word she could choke out.

"Where else?" He gave her a chilling smile. "The Flying W."

Chapter Seventeen

Night offered no relief from the heat of the day. The performance seemed to move in slow motion, taking longer than ever to complete. All the while, Jack's sense that something was wrong grew until trepidation sat on his heart like a concrete block. The second the applause exploded behind him, he turned the Appaloosa down a side street and rode it to the stable. Milling tourists impeded his progress through town, but before returning to the motel, he searched the Golden Broom for Red and Duke.

Neither was anywhere to be seen, and his anxiety had mushroomed into full-blown apprehension by the time he entered the motel office. The tinkle of the bell scratched his nerve endings. Cats stirred at his intrusion, but paid him little heed. "Minna! Andy!"

Minna appeared in the hallway. Worry tugged at her feline features. "I thought ya was Andy returnin'."

"What do you mean, returning?" His pulse lurched, then kicked into a gallop. "Where did she go?"

"Well, I ain't certain. I told her to stay put whilst I checked in a nice family from Minnesota, but after I showed 'em to their cabin, I noticed that red station wagon of hers turnin' down the road."

Fear lanced Jack's heart. He hadn't seen the Cherokee. It hadn't come down Main Street—unless she'd driven out that way while he was at the stable. "Which direction did she go?"

Minna pointed. "Toward the mountain."

Toward the Flying W. But why? "She promised she wouldn't go anywhere without me."

"All I know is she was awful upset about not bein' able to recollect who Nightmare Man was. I tried gettin' her mind on other stuff so as it could jest come back to her on its own, but she was awful antsy."

"Damn. She must have thought that going out to the ranch at night would help her remember."

"Don't seem like somethin' she'd do if'n she promised ya she'd wait fer ya."

"No, it doesn't…." The hair on his nape prickled. "Maybe she didn't go of her own accord."

"Oh, my." Minna's cat eyes rounded in fear. "You think someone snuck in whilst I was helpin' the Minnesota family?"

"Did you see whether or not she was alone in the Cherokee?"

Minna shook her head. "No."

The blood in Jack's veins felt icy. "Get me a rifle!"

"A rifle? Oh, my." Minna moved with a speed Jack would never have suspected her of having, hurriedly pulling a rifle from the rack and a box of shells from a locked cupboard beneath it. She said, "We can't let nothin' happen to Andy."

"No, we can't." Fear tasted metallic on his tongue. If Andy really had a guardian angel, Jack prayed that angel was watching over her now.

OH GRAM, WHY didn't I remember in time to expose him? Desolation and terror controlled Andy, zapping her spirit, her strength to fight back. She was going to die. The future she'd fantasized with Jack would never be. The justice she'd wanted for her parents, for Jack's father, for Wally and Coop and

Karen Bradley would never happen. Bile climbed the back of her throat and slid across her tongue. *I've let you down, Gram. I've let us all down.*

The light from the Cherokee's headlights bobbed against the terrain. She gripped the steering wheel so tightly her fingers ached as she drove through the welcome arch and up to the burned-out foundation of the house. He yanked on her hair, the huge metal bird claw once more at her throat. "Stop here."

Andy complied, a small whimper escaping her. Then she stiffened, hearing Gram's voice as sharp inside her head as a slap. *Stop feeling sorry for yourself, Andrea Hart. Use that brain of yours for something constructive. You've outwitted this one before. Do it again. Because if you don't—he'll go after your Jack when he's finished with you.*

The truth of this shot through Andy like a jolt of adrenaline. She damn well would not let Nightmare Man hurt Jack—not even if it took her dying to save him.

Nightmare Man twisted her hair tighter. "Get out of the car."

Tears stung her eyes at the pain in her scalp. Awkwardly, they emerged into the night. The rising moon shone down on the homestead as huge as a supper plate in the sky, as full as it had been that awful night twenty years earlier. The air was cool this near the mountains, but sweat trickled down Andy's spine.

A horse whinnied, startling her. She jerked toward the sound and saw the animal tethered to a nearby alder tree. Immediately she realized its purpose—his escape.

"I take it you plan on making it look as if I drove out here and met with a fatal accident—something like Wally Lester."

"Clever girl. I find tedious explanations a bore." He shoved her to the ground, his strength incredible, in part from hours in the gym, in part from insanity.

Andy crawled to the concrete foundation, then turned and

stared at him. He was dressed all in black, including a ski mask rolled up on his head, hiding his white-white hair. In the moonlight, Gene Mott looked a creature of the night, his pale skin iridescent, ghostly, his paler eyes empty sockets in a skull.

His voice dripped with hatred. "At long last, I will be able to leave this town and quit pretending I can't walk. I believe I shall go to Switzerland and claim some miracle surgery."

Andy strove to delay the inevitable. There were all kinds of objects in the debris-littered foundation. If she could distract him, she could surely find something for a weapon. "My mother *was* the woman you were in love with."

"Ah, the beautiful Marcy. She was kind to me. For a time. Your father and I both met her at college, but until the night I confessed my love to her, I didn't know she found me repulsive. She was such a clever liar, I'd never even guessed."

He looked dazed, as if he were remembering. Andy used the moment to slip up and onto the edge of the foundation. She dipped her hand into the refuse heap behind her and scrounged for something solid with some heft.

"I only wanted a kiss. One little kiss. What carnage it led to. You understand I couldn't just leave it like that. I had to destroy the evidence." He focused on her again and even in the indistinct light she could see the hatred in his eyes. "You should have stayed in bed. You should have died."

He started toward her. Moonlight flashed off the bronze-coated bird talon.

Andy scrambled over the foundation and stepped out of his reach. The footing was uneven. Each step awkward. She had to keep him talking. "I remembered you were Nightmare Man before you arrived tonight. I told Minna. She'll tell Jack and the sheriff. They'll arrest you."

"For what? An accident? The sheriff cannot arrest me on the word of a woman so distraught she drove to a deserted ranch in the dark of night."

"They'll know I wouldn't come out here alone at night."

"But they won't be able to prove it."

The sound of a vehicle bumping down the road at high speed reached them. Hope leapt inside Andy. Mott lunged at her, slashing with the talon. She lurched to the side. The talon swung through empty air, missing her by mere inches.

Headlights stroked the night sky. "It's too late. Help is coming."

"No, it's too late for you."

Andy's foot hit something solid. Losing her balance, she fell back and landed hard on her fanny. Her legs rested atop Gram's kettle. Grasping it to her like a shield, she warded off the bird claw as it knifed toward her again. Metal clanged against metal.

Mott swore. The headlights swept over them. He ducked his head, dragging the ski mask over his face, keeping his back toward the approaching pickup, obviously thinking he could still get away.

The vehicle stopped just under the welcome arch. Mott came at Andy again. She jerked back, lifting the kettle. Beneath her, the flooring bowed. A new fear speared Andy. She stilled, remembering the cellar full of snakes. Mott growled and swung his arm downward. Andy batted at him with the kettle.

The crack of a rifle rang out. Mott's body jerked. He pitched forward. Andy curled into a ball. Mott rolled over her, landing behind her with a thud. She tasted soot and grime and absolute terror. For a split second all was silent. Then the sound of disturbed diamondbacks rent the quietude. Andy's heart crawled into her throat.

She inched away from Mott. He groaned and reached for her, catching the hem of her shirt. Without warning the floor beneath him imploded, dragging Mott down. He held tight to Andy's blouse. She felt herself being sucked backward. The top button of her blouse rode up to choke her. She gasped, jerked at the next three buttons and inched backward.

Fabric ripped. Suddenly she was free. She leapt to her feet and out of the foundation right into Jack's arms. Minna appeared at Jack's side, holding a rifle. "I didn't hit him nowheres vital, but I'm afraid them snakes did."

Jack nodded. "The sheriff is on his way."

THE SHERIFF ARRIVED too late for Gene Mott, but he let Jack sit in as he questioned everyone. The next day as he watched Andy pack her suitcase, Jack told her what he knew. "Cliff had suspected his uncle could walk. However, he'd never caught him at it. But he was devastated to learn the man he'd idolized was a liar and a murderer."

Andy felt sorry for Cliff. "I imagine he has some hard times ahead with the publicity and the stigma that will be attached to his name."

"He's in good hands. Immediately recognizing a candidate for her frustrated mothering, Minna took him in tow."

"What about Duke?" Andy closed her suitcase and started filling her book bag.

Jack leaned against the desk. "He owned up to giving Mott a scorpion. But it took a while before he admitted he'd known for years that Gene could walk. Claimed he kept the secret because he felt sorry for him—some lame excuse about their being blood brothers as kids. Frankly, I think Mott had something on him, was blackmailing him, but of course he'll never admit that."

"What about the welt above Red's eye?" She shoved the dictionary into the bag and zipped the closure.

"While he was trying to help Wally, he knocked his head against the doorframe."

"I guess we owe him an apology for suspecting him."

"I wouldn't waste any sympathy on Red. He was as stunned as any of them to learn about Gene. But the moment it sank in, and he realized sightseers will likely show up to see where the famous author-murderer lived and died—there were dollar signs in his eyes. I swear. He offered Cliff and Minna four times what they paid for the Flying W.''

"Well, I don't want to earn money from other people's unhappiness.'' Andy moved to the bed, giving the room one last glance to make certain she hadn't forgotten anything. One day she would use her experiences in Alder Gulch in a novel—not the actual events, but the emotions. She didn't know how her writing would be affected, but it would be. From here on, her life would be different. She had a new identity, a new perspective, a new reason for living.

She lifted her suitcase from the bed. If her future was so rosy, why did her heart feel as heavy as her luggage? But of course she knew. She was returning to Seattle—and Jack was helping her load the Cherokee as if he couldn't get rid of her fast enough.

For the first time in fifteen years, Jack felt like a free man. His obsession was ended, but instead of being happy, he ached from the inside of his heart to the depths of his soul. Andy was returning to Seattle, and he didn't know how to stop her. Didn't know if he should stop her. He tucked her big suitcase into the rear of the Cherokee. "What are you going to do now?''

"Try and finish my book while my editor is still in a generous mood.'' She sounded as if it would be a chore, the enthusiasm she'd expressed earlier for the book gone.

"I see.'' Jack nodded, but a sadness—which she had expected would vanish with his obsession—still lingered in his eyes.

She handed him her laptop computer. "What about you?''

He placed her computer beside her suitcase, then lifted his Stetson and raked his fingers through his hair. "The *Sun* will need someone to write this story, and I owe it to Wally to be that someone.''

"He'd like that."

Andy settled her overnight case beside the rest of her luggage and closed the hatch, then moved to the driver's door.

Jack caught her arm gently. She gazed into his sage green eyes, wondering if she'd ever get over him.

Jack gazed into her beautifully unique eyes, wondering how he'd stand not being able to look into them every day. "Andy, what about us?"

"Don't worry, Jack, I won't hold you to anything." Sadness and confusion clashed in her eyes.

He scowled, not understanding their source. "What if I want to be held to something?"

Her heart leapt into her throat. "Do you?"

He kissed her gently on the lips. "I love you, lady."

He thought his heart would break as he waited for her to respond. Had she realized it was really her former fiancé who held her heart? Would she say she didn't know who or what she wanted?

The sadness and confusion left her eyes, tears taking their place. "I love you, too, cowboy."

Jack released his breath and pulled her into his arms. He gazed down at her, gently brushing her tears with the pads of his thumbs. "Do you suppose this story could have a happy ending?"

"Well, I can't speak for you, but my stories always end with my heroines knowing who the right man is."

"Am *I* the right man?"

"Hmm?" She looked over his shoulder, glancing heavenward. "What do you think, Gram? Is Jack the right man for me?" Andy smiled at Gram's answer. Then she smiled at Jack. "My darling, Gram says, 'You're a fool if you can't see that.'"

Harlequin Romance®

Delightful
Affectionate
Romantic
Emotional

Tender
Original

Daring
Riveting
Enchanting
Adventurous
Moving

Harlequin Romance®—
capturing the world you dream of...

Harlequin® Historical

From rugged lawmen and valiant knights to defiant heiresses and spirited frontierswomen, Harlequin Historicals will capture your imagination with their dramatic scope, passion and adventure.

Harlequin Historicals . . . they're too good to miss!

Where love comes alive™

From first love to forever, these love stories are
for today's woman with traditional values.

A highly passionate, emotionally powerful
and always provocative read.

Silhouette®

SPECIAL EDITION™

Emotional, compelling stories that capture the
intensity of living, loving and creating a family in
today's world.

Silhouette®

INTIMATE MOMENTS™

A roller-coaster read that delivers romantic thrills
in a world of suspense, adventure and more.

HARLEQUIN®
Presents

The world's bestselling romance series...
The series that brings you your favorite authors,
month after month:

Helen Bianchin...Emma Darcy
Lynne Graham...Penny Jordan
Miranda Lee...Sandra Marton
Anne Mather...Carole Mortimer
Susan Napier...Michelle Reid

and many more uniquely talented authors!

Wealthy, powerful, gorgeous men...
Women who have feelings just like your own...
The stories you love, set in exotic, glamorous locations...

HARLEQUIN®
Presents

Seduction and Passion Guaranteed!

HPDIR104